THE DEVIL IN THE HILLS

CESARE PAVESE

THE DEVIL IN THE HILLS

TRANSLATED FROM THE ITALIAN BY
D.D. PAIGE

PETER OWEN
LONDON AND CHESTER SPRINGS

PETER OWEN LTD
73 Kenway Road, London SW5 0RE

Peter Owen books are distributed in the USA by
Dufour Editions Inc., Chester Springs, PA 19425-0007

First British Commonwealth edition 1954
This paperback edition 2002
English translation © Peter Owen Ltd 1954

Translated from the Italian *Il Diavolo sulle colline*

A catalogue record for this book is available from
the British Library

ISBN 0 7206 1118 0

Printed and bound in Great Britain by
Bookmarque Ltd, Croydon, Surrey

THE DEVIL IN THE HILLS

1

We were very young. I believe I never slept that year. But I had a friend who slept even less than I did, and certain mornings you would see him strolling about in front of the station during the hour in which the first trains arrive and depart. We used to leave him late at night, on his doorstep; Pieretto would take another walk and even see the dawn in, and then drink his coffee. Now he was studying the sleepy faces of streetsweepers and cyclists. Even he could not remember the discussions of the previous night: but having stayed awake on them, he had digested them, and he said calmly: "It's late. I'm going to bed."

Some of the others who tagged along after us couldn't understand what we did when the cinemas were closed, and the clubs, the inns and the conversation at an end. They would sit on the benches with the three of us, listen to us shout or cackle, become fired with the idea of going to wake up the girls or to await the dawn on the hills, then at our change of mood they would hesitate and find the courage to go home. The next day they would ask us: "What did you do afterwards?" It wasn't an easy question to answer. We had listened to a drunk, watched the posters being pasted up, taken a walk through the Market, seen sheep pass along the avenues. Then Pieretto would say: "We met a woman."

They wouldn't believe us and yet they weren't able to contradict us.

"You need perseverance," Pieretto would say. "You walk up and down under her balcony. All night: she knows it, she becomes aware of it. You don't even have to know her; she feels it in her blood. The moment comes when she can't stand it any longer, she jumps from her bed and opens the shutters for you. You lean the ladder against. . . ."

But when we three were alone, we didn't like to talk about women. At least, not seriously. Neither Pieretto nor Oreste told me everything about themselves. That was why I liked them. Women, the sort who separate old friends, would come later. Now we talked only about the world, the rain and the sun; and we enjoyed it so much that going home to sleep really seemed like a waste of time.

One night that year we were on the avenue by the banks of the Po, seated on a bench. Oreste had mumbled: "Let's go to bed."

"Why don't you turn in here?" we said. "Why waste the summer? Don't you know how to sleep with one eye open?"

Oreste, his cheek resting on the back of the bench, watched us circumspectly.

I said that one should never sleep in the city. "It's never dark, always daytime. One ought to do something every night."

"That's because you're children," Pieretto said. "You're children and you're greedy."

"And you?" I said. "I suppose you're an old man?"

Oreste jumped up unexpectedly: "They say old men never sleep . . . And we walk around all night. I'd like to know who does sleep."

Pieretto smiled sarcastically.

"What is it?" I asked cautiously.

"If you want to sleep, first you need a woman," Pieretto said. "That's why neither you nor the old men sleep."

"That may be," Oreste mumbled, "but I'm dropping from sleep just the same."

"You're not city-bred," Pieretto remarked. "Night still means something to someone like you, means what it used to mean. You're like watchdogs or chickens."

It was past two. On the other side of the Po, the hill sparkled.

We got up and climbed towards the centre. I meditated on Pieretto's strange ability to be so sure of himself and make us consider ourselves innocents. Neither Oreste nor I, for example, lost much thought over women. For the nth time I wondered what sort of life Pieretto had lived before coming to Turin.

On the benches by the station flower-beds, under the meagre shadow of one of those little trees, two beggars slept with their mouths open. In shirt sleeves, unshaven and curly-haired, they resembled gypsies. The public convenience is only a few steps away, and for all the night's savour of freshness and summer, there reigned in that place a musty smell, a sourness, which recalled the long day of sun and movement and uproar, of sweat and warm asphalt, of seething crowds. Towards evening little old women, street pedlars, the uprooted, always sat on those benches— thin oases in the heart of Turin—; and they were bored, they waited, they grew old. What were they waiting for? Pieretto said that they were waiting for something enormous, the collapse of the city, the apocalypse. Sometimes a summer storm drives them away and washes everything clean.

9

The pair that night slept like the dead. In the square some of the electric advertisements still spoke to the empty sky, throwing their light on the two dead men.

"They've settled in for the night," Oreste said. "That's what we ought to do."

He moved off to go away.

"Come along with us," Pieretto said; "there's nobody waiting for you at home."

"And there's nobody waiting for you where you're going either," Oreste said, but he came along just the same.

We took the street towards the new porticoes. "Those two. . . ." I said quietly. "It must be beautiful to wake up in the sun in the square."

Pieretto said nothing.

"Where are we going?" I asked, stopping.

Pieretto went ahead a couple of steps and then stopped.

"I could understand going somewhere," I said. "But everything's closed now. There's not a soul about. . . . I wonder what use all these lights have."

Pieretto didn't say, as he ordinarily would have, "Do *you* have any use?" But instead he muttered: "Do you want to go up the hill?"

"It's far," I said.

"It's far, but it has that wonderful odour," he said.

We went down the wide avenue again; crossing the bridge I felt cold; then we started up the path at a brisk pace in order to get out of the familiar districts. It was damp, dark, moonless; fireflies flashed. After a bit we slowed down, sweating. As we walked along we talked about our work, our experiences, our futures. We talked about ourselves with enthusiasm, we even drew Oreste into the conversation; we had walked through those streets other times, warmed by wine or by the company; but none of this mattered, it was a pretext for walking, for having the bulk of the hill beneath our feet. We walked among fields, boundary walls, gates of villas; we breathed the asphalt and the woods.

"To me, there's no difference between this and a cut flower," Pieretto said.

Though it may seem strange, we had never gone up to the crest, at least not by the road. There was probably a place there, a gap, where the road became level, the last levelling of the slope, which I imagined as a final hedge, a balcony open to the external world of the plain. From other spots on the hills, from Superga, from Pino, we had already looked on the other side, in full day. Oreste had pointed to his town on the horizon of that sea of scattered houses and vague, wooded shadows.

"It's really late," Oreste said. "Before, there used to be night clubs round here."

"They have closing hours, you know," Pieretto said. "But people already inside can stay on."

"It's hardly worth the while to come up the hill in the summer," I said, "just to drink and dance behind closed doors and shutters."

"They probably have gardens," Oreste said. "Fields. They probably sleep in the park."

"There comes a time when the parks get filled up," I said. "Then there are woods and vineyards."

Oreste grunted.

I said to Pieretto: "You don't know the country. You walk around all night but you don't know the country."

11

Pieretto did not reply. Now and then a dog barked somewhere.

"Let's stop," Oreste said, at a turn in the road.

Pieretto came out of his thoughts. "How should I?" he said quickly, "since snakes and hares have gone underground and are afraid of the passers by? The chief odour here is the petrol. Does the countryside you like so much really exist any more? And if so, where?" He fastened on me savagely. "If someone happened to have his throat cut in the woods," he declared in his peremptory tone, "do you really believe that it would be like something out of a legend? That the crickets would fall silent around the corpse? That the puddle of blood would matter more than some spittle?"

Oreste, waiting, spat with disgust. He said: "Look out, a car is coming down the road."

A large, pale green, open car appeared slowly and silently and stopped without a jar, docilely. The rear half remained in the shadow under the trees. We looked at it surprised.

"The headlights are out," Oreste said.

I thought that there was a couple inside and I would have preferred to have been far away, on the gap, and not have met anyone. Why didn't they shoot off in that marvel of theirs and go to Turin and leave us alone in our countryside? Oreste, his head down, suggested we move along.

Brushing past the car, I expected to hear whispers and rustling, laughter even, but instead I caught sight of a man alone at the wheel, a young man with his face twisted up towards the sky.

"He looks dead," Pieretto said.

Oreste was already out of the shadow. We walked along,

accompanied by the noise of crickets; and during my few steps under the trees, I thought of many things. I did not dare turn round. Pieretto was silent beside me. The tension became intolerable. I stopped.

"It's impossible," I said. "That chap's not sleeping."

"What are you afraid of?" Pieretto said.

"Did you see him?"

"He was sleeping."

I said that no one falls asleep like that in a moving car. Pieretto's attack still rang in my ears. "If only some one would come along." We turned round to watch the curve, black with trees. A firefly crossed the road, brightening like a cigarette.

"Let's wait and hear if he starts off."

Pieretto said that anyone who had a car like that could do as he pleased and look at the stars. I kept my ear cocked. "Perhaps he's seen us."

"Let's see if he replies," Oreste said, and he gave a shout. Lacerating, bestial, it began like a roar and filled the earth and sky, the bellow of a bull which then faded out in a drunken laugh. Oreste jumped out of the way of my kick. We all kept our ears cocked. The dog barked again, the crickets went silent, terrified. Nothing. Oreste opened his mouth to give the cry again and Pieretto said "All together now."

This time we bellowed in unison, for a long time, with strident returns and responses. My skin crawled, and I thought that, like the ray of a headlight in the night, the sound reached everywhere—the slopes, the bottom of the paths, the clots of shadow, entered the dens and penetrated roots, making everything vibrate.

13

Again the dog went wild. We listened, staring at the curve. I was about to say "He must have died of fright," when we heard the door of the car close with a thud. Oreste said into my ear: "Now the Road Patrol will be along," and we waited, watching the trees. But for a time there was nothing. By now the dog was quiet, and the crickets' chirping spread everywhere under the stars. We stared at the band of shadow.

"Come on," I said, "there are three of us."

2

We found him seated on the footboard, his face in his hands. He didn't move. We stood looking at him from a few paces off, as though he were a dangerous beast.

"Do you think he's being sick?" Pieretto said.

"We'll see," Oreste said. He went close to him and put a palm against his forehead, as one does to feel fever. The other pressed against Oreste's hand, like a dog playing. They had an air of shoving one another away, and I felt that they were smiling ironically. Oreste turned round.

"It's Poli," he said. "I know that much. They have a villa near us."

The other, seated, held one of Oreste's hands and wiped his face like a person coming out of the water. He was a handsome young man somewhat older than us, with circled, terrified eyes. Holding onto Oreste's hand, he looked at us without any indication that he saw us.

It was then that Oreste said to him: "Weren't you supposed to be in Milan?"

"There's still time to flush a few more coverts," the other said. "Have you come squirrel hunting?"

"We're not at the Coste," Oreste said and freed his hand. Then, looking closely at the car, he said: "You have a new one?"

"Why should he try to talk sense with a drunk?" I thought. My earlier fright had turned into irritation. "Why doesn't he leave him in the ditch?"

The Devil in the Hills

That chap Poli looked at us. He resembled those sick people who stare from their beds, terrified and sorrowful. None of us had ever been in such a state. And yet he was tanned and in every way looked as though he went with such a car. I felt ashamed of our earlier catcall.

"Can't you see Turin from here?" he said, getting quickly to his feet and looking round. "You ought to be able to. Can you see Turin?"

If it hadn't been for his voice, which seemed thick, raucous and weak at the same time, you would have thought him now almost normal. He looked round and said to Oreste: "I came here three nights ago. There's a place near here that you can see Turin from. Do you want to come along? It's a beautiful place."

We formed a group, and Oreste asked him suddenly: "Have you run away from home?"

"Some people are waiting for me in Turin," he said. "*Nouveaux riches,* unbearable people." He looked at us, smiling like a shamed child. "They're really disgusting, these people who wear gloves all the time. Even when conceiving children or making their millions."

Pieretto, standing close beside him, looked at him out of the corner of his eye.

The other took out a packet of cigarettes and passed them round. They were soft, toasted. We lit up.

"If they saw me with you and your friends," Poli said, "they'd laugh. I find it amusing to drop people like that."

Pieretto said loudly: "It doesn't take much to amuse you."

Poli said: "I like to have my little jokes. Don't you?"

"If you want to speak badly of people who have made

16

money," Pieretto said, "you should know how to make money too. Or else live without spending tuppence."

Then Poli, with a disturbed expression, said: "Do you really think so?" He said it so seriously that even Oreste couldn't keep back a smile. Immediately Poli, stretching out his arms, gathered us together with an air of making us accomplices. He said in a very low voice: "There's another reason."

"Go ahead."

Poli let his arms drop and sighed. He looked at us humbly, from the depths of his eyes, and really seemed in a bad way.

"It's that I feel like a god tonight," he said softly.

No one laughed. There was an instant of silence, and Oreste said: "Let's go and see Turin."

We went down a bit of road, to a terrace on a curve from which you could see the dazzle of Turin. We stopped at the edge of the embankment. When the three of us had come up the hill, we had never once turned round. Poli, with his arm on Oreste's shoulder, looked at the sea of lights. He threw away his cigarette and looked.

"Well. What shall we do now?" Oreste said.

"How small man is!" Poli said. "Alleys, court-yards, roof-tops. Seen from here it's like a sea of stars. And yet when you're down there you don't notice it at all."

Pieretto went off a couple of paces. Watering a bush, he shouted: "You're just stringing us."

And Poli calmly replied: "I like the contrast. It's only in contrasts that one feels himself stronger, superior to his own body. Life is banal without contrasts. I have no illusions."

"Is there anyone who does?" Oreste asked.

The other raised his eyes and smiled. "Why, everyone. All the people sleeping in those houses. They think they're somebody, they dream, they wake up, they make love, 'I'm so-and-so and such-and-such' and instead.· . . ."

"Instead what?" Pieretto said, coming back.

Poli, having been interrupted, had lost the thread. He cracked his fingers, searching for words.

"You were saying that life is boring," Oreste said.

"Life is what we are," Pieretto said.

Poli said: "Let's sit down." He didn't seem drunk at all. I began to believe that those troubled eyes of his were like his silk shirt, his handshake, his fine car—the things habitual to him and inseparable from him.

We chatted for a while, seated on the grass. I let them talk, listening to the crickets. Poli seemed to pay no attention to Pieretto's sarcastic remarks: he explained to him why he had fled Turin and human society for three nights; he mentioned hotels, important people, kept women. As fast as Pieretto warmed up to him and accepted him, I drew off from him: I convinced myself that he was only an innocent. I fell into the humour I had been in when the car had stopped and I had imagined that there were people making love inside.

Suddenly I said: "It seems pointless to come up here from Turin and then never leave off talking about the city."

"Of course! He's right," Oreste said, jumping to his feet. "Let's go home, tomorrow we have to work."

Poli got up and Pieretto followed. "Aren't you coming?" they asked me.

As we walked towards the car, I held back with Oreste and asked him about Poli. He told me that Poli's family had estates near his place, a large villa, an entire hill. "When he was a boy, he used to come into the country and we hunted together. He was undisciplined then, but he didn't drink like this."

He shouted to Poli: "Are you going to the Greppo this year?"

Poli ended his discussion with Pieretto and turned round.

"Dad locked me up there last year and took the car away from me," he said without any embarrassment. "People have strange ideas. He wanted to get me away from—— From what. . . .? I don't know if I'm going back there. It might be nice to spend a day there, that's all, with some friends and some records."

He opened the doors with a gesture of invitation. I should have preferred not to get in because I realized that we couldn't be ourselves with him. We had to listen to him and accept his word, and reply in the same manner. To be courteous to him meant that you had to be his reflection. I couldn't understand how Oreste had managed to stay in his company for days.

Poli turned round from the wheel and said: "Well, are we going?"

"Where?"

"To the Greppo."

Oreste jumped in. "Are we crazy? I want to go to sleep."

I also protested that it was an absurd hour.

"It's not day yet," Poli said. It's three-something. We'll get there at five."

Together we shouted that we had to go home. "Take us into town," Oreste said. "There'll be another time."

"Can we trust him?" I asked Oreste.

Oreste said: "I want to go to sleep. Leave us off at Porta Nuova."

We started off for Turin. The car sped easily, surely. Pieretto, seated in front with Poli, hadn't said anything.

We were on the lighted and abandoned avenues. Oreste got out in Via Nizza, in front of the porticoes. Standing on the footboard, he said good-bye to Poli. After a moment they dropped me off at my door. I said good-bye. I told Pieretto we would meet the next day. The car vanished with the two of them.

3

During the day we sweated over certain exams; especially Oreste, who was studying medicine. Pieretto and I were preparing for law and we had postponed the big push to October: as everyone knows, law is mainly improvisation and you can't go at it scientifically. Oreste, on the other hand, was swotting hard and didn't always come out with us in the evening. But we knew where to find him during the early afternoon: he had a house in the country, but he rented a room in Turin and ate in restaurants.

I spent the day after that evening looking for him. I found him in the restaurant, nibbling at an apple, his elbow on his briefcase, his back against the wall. He asked me, in the mugginess of the restaurant, if I had seen Pieretto.

Fanning ourselves, we talked about the plans we had made for that year. The three of us were to have a country holiday at Oreste's place; his farm was large and we would have fun there. But Pieretto and I had the idea of throwing our knapsacks on our shoulders and going on foot. Oreste said it was silly: once we arrived we would get our fill both of the country and the heat.

"Where's Pieretto?"

"You don't think he went to bed last night, do you?" Oreste said.

"Perhaps he's studying."

"Like the devil," Oreste said. "When there's Poli and his car? Didn't you see how well they got along together?"

Then we talked about the night before, about Poli, about how strange it all was. Oreste said there was nothing to be astonished about. He was an old friend and not just an acquaintance of Poli, even though the latter's father was an extraordinarily wealthy man, a *commendatore* from Milan, who owned that enormous estate that he never used. Poli had grown up there, summer after summer, with ten nursemaids and a carriage and horses, and only when he put on his first long trousers had he been able to have his say and go out and meet people in the towns round about. For two or three seasons, when the woodcocks were flying, he had gone shooting with Oreste's crowd. He was a good kid and had a head on his shoulders. He lacked only perseverence; that, definitely. Half-way through something, he would change his mind.

"It's the sort of life they lead," I said. "They become like women."

"He's got understanding, however," Oreste said. "You heard what he says about his own sort?"

"He says that just for something to say. He was drunk."

Here Oreste shook his head. He said that Poli wasn't drunk. A drunk is different. "He might have been drunk for three days and done something swinish. But now he was much worse. A chap likes a drunk." Oreste occasionally had these unexpected observations.

"He didn't really have it in for his sort. He had it in for those who've made money and don't know how to spend it," I said. "You're his friend. You ought to know that."

"You know how it is," Oreste said. "Going hunting together is like going to school together. . . . My father always liked me to hunt."

He finished his wine and we left. As we passed a block of houses in the sun, I pointed out that Pieretto had probably said all sorts of extravagant things to Poli. "Pieretto has that way of laughing which seems as though he's spitting in your face. He doesn't notice it, but he offends people".

"I wonder . . ." Oreste said. "I've never seen Poli offended."

Neither Pieretto nor Oreste came out that evening. Sometimes when I was alone that year, I would go through some ugly moments. Going home to study was senseless; I was too accustomed to live and argue with Pieretto and wander about the streets; in the air, in the movement, even in the dark of the avenues there were more things than I could understand and enjoy. I was always on the point of approaching a girl or slipping into a dubious dive or deciding to start off on an avenue and walk until daylight and at the end find myself heaven knows where. Instead, I would walk round in the usual streets, cross and recross, at the same corners under the same street-signs and see the same faces. At times I would stop, irresolute, on a corner and remain there for half an hour at a time in a fury against myself.

But that particular evening things went better with me. The recent meeting with Poli had torn away many of my scruples and I told myself that there were privileged people more absurd than myself, useless people, who, day and night, enjoyed themselves more than I. For, without knowing it, my father and mother, provincials moved to the city, had inculcated this in me: the mad acts of the poor will be permitted you, those of the rich, never. Of course, poor doesn't mean utterly ragged.

The Devil in the Hills

I spent the evening in a cinema, amused, but my thoughts occupied by Poli. When I got out, I wasn't sleepy and I walked in the fresh air, along the deserted streets under the stars. I was born in Turin and had always lived there, but that evening I thought about the narrow paths of my parents' town, paths which led through the countryside. And Oreste lived in a similar town and would soon return. Return and remain. That was his ambition. If he wanted, he could remain in the city. But what was the difference?

When I got to my door, someone called me. It was Pieretto, who, coming out of the shadow of the wall, crossed the street and approached me. He wanted to stay a while and talk, he wasn't sleepy yet. He hadn't been round earlier in the evening because he had spent the whole day with Poli. The night before they had ended by touring the country; in the morning they had found themselves at the lakes, under the sun; there Poli had been ill, he had fallen like a sack on getting out of the car: perhaps it had been the blinding sunlight. He was full of cocain. Poli was, poisoned. Then Pieretto had telephoned that hotel in Turin; someone had answered that he should telephone Milan. "I haven't any money," Pieretto had shouted into the mouthpiece. Then a priest who knew how to drive got into the car and they took Poli to Novara. Here a doctor had woken him up, made him sweat and vomit; then they argued with the priest, who had accused Pieretto of having been Poli's evil genius. In the end, Poli had arranged everything, paid the doctor, the telephone call and the lunch; and they had taken the priest back home, giving him a long lecture on sin and on hell.

Pieretto was completely happy. He had enjoyed Poli's lunacy, enjoyed the trip, enjoyed the priest's face. Now Poli had gone to bathe and change; there was some woman mixed up in it, a sort of fury, who had followed him from Milan to Turin and besieged him in his hotel, she wanted to talk with him and sent him flowers.

"Perhaps he is a bit of an ass," Pieretto said, "but he knows how to enjoy himself. He has a good time for the money he spends."

"He goes too far," I said; "he's irresponsible."

Then Pieretto set himself to explain that Poli did no worse than we did. Uprooted and *bourgeois*, we spent the night arguing on benches, we hired prostitutes, drank wine; but he had other means at his disposal, he had drugs, complete freedom, high-class women. Wealth is power. That's all.

"You're crazy," I said. "We do think a bit. I want to know why I have a good time when I take a walk. For example, you haunt Turin and I like to go up Superga. I like the smell of the earth. Why? Poli doesn't give a damn about these things. He's an irresponsible, Oreste says so too."

"You're both a couple of asses," Pieretto shot back; and he explained that people have need of experience and of danger and that your limits are imposed by the environment you live in. "Perhaps Poli does say and do foolish things," he said, "perhaps all he leaves for us is the dry bones. But he wouldn't be as happy if he lived as we do."

We began to walk along, arguing as we usually did. Pieretto maintained that Poli was quite right in seeking to know life according to his means.

"But when he talks stupidities. . . ." I objected.

"It doesn't matter," Pieretto said. "In his own way, he

works very hard and touches things which you others don't even suspect."

"Does he want you to take coke too?"

Irritated, Pieretto said that Poli didn't make a pose of the drug. He mentioned it seldom. But he had told that priest things about sin which revealed a profound eye and a true experience. Then I laughed at Pieretto, and he became irritated again.

"You're scandalized because someone takes coke," he said, "and then you laugh when he talks about sin?"

He stopped in front of a bar. He said that he was going to telephone. After a bit he leaned out of the telephone-box, he wanted to know if Oreste was coming.

"It's midnight. Oreste is sleeping. That's what *his* means necessitate," I said.

Pieretto shouted into the telephone. He continued for a bit. He smiled ironically as he talked. When he came out he said: "We're going to Poli's."

4

The idea of spending another white night terrified me. My father and mother wouldn't say anything; perhaps a couple of words at the time, a glance upwards from their plates, cautious questions about the examination schedule. I don't know how Pieretto managed with his parents; but the defenceless faces of mine hurt me, and I wondered what sort of chap my father had been at twenty and what sort of girl my mother had been and whether one fine day I too should have children so different from me as I from them. Probably my parents thought of the turf in the public gardens, women, the antecamera of the gaol. What did they know about our nocturnal manias? Or perhaps they were right: it's always a matter of boredom and then of an initial vice, and everything is born from that.

When we were in front of the hotel with Rosalba, who paced up and down, and Poli manœuvred the car so that we could get in, I muttered to Pieretto: "A definite understanding tonight. It's already midnight."

It was obvious that Poli wanted us with him in order to limit the woman's expansiveness. In fact, he said so, with a little joke. He had introduced us to her as "the best in Turin": she should listen and learn. In Poli's world people are very caddish: they treat each other with gay effrontery. I couldn't understand why Pieretto should lend himself to such a game.

Rosalba got in front with Poli. She was a thin woman, poor thing, with red eyes and a stiff carriage, she wore a flower in her hair. She couldn't keep still, and before, while we were waiting, she gave us troubled glances, tried to smile and looked at herself in the mirror. She wore a pink evening gown and might have passed for Poli's mother.

He joked and told us a thousand things. He looked at the woman with brisk eyes, laughed and steered expertly. In an instant we were out of Turin. Pieretto, leaning forward, said something to him.

Poli braked suddenly. We were in the black country, in front of the mountains. Rosalba laughed, excited.

"Where are we going?"

I said unambiguously that I didn't intend to stay out all night.

Poli turned round and said to me: "I'd like you to keep us company. Trust us. We won't be out late."

The woman said desolately: "Let's stop, Poli. Why do you want to drive all night? You're always so rash."

Poli started the engine again. Before throwing the car into gear, he murmured to the woman. I saw the two heads together and distinguished the eagerness and intimacy of their voices, then her head nodded energetically. Poli turned round and smiled at us.

He turned the car round in the street and we started back to Turin. Speeding along the deserted avenues on the outskirts, we came to the hill, black in the night. Then, beneath its flanks, we ran along the Po. We passed Sassi. It was clear that Poli and Rosalba had already been in that district. She pressed close to his shoulder. What did Pieretto see in those two? I wondered if she knew about Poli's drugs, I tried to imagine them together, drunk, to detest them. But I didn't succeed. For the strangeness of that drive, the jouncing of the car in the night, the black water and the black hill above us kept my mind off everything else.

"Here! Here we are!" Rosalba shouted, and Poli was slowing down in front of an illuminated villa. He turned onto the gravel drive and stopped in the car park. In front of the villa, set above the river bank, there was an open space, half-dark, with tables and discreet shaded lamps. I saw the white coats of waiters.

After the commotion and embarrassment of sitting down and ordering was over—Rosalba changed her mind a number of times, wouldn't listen to anyone's suggestions, became sulky and talked loudly; Pieretto put his elbows on the table, showing his frayed cuffs—after all that, I decided to let them talk among themselves and said to myself: "After all, it's just like any ordinary café." I relaxed against the back of the chair and cocked my ear towards the shadow to try to hear the water.

But it wasn't just like any ordinary café. A small orchestra began with a crash, and then immediately played softly, and in the centre of the circle of tables a woman appeared and sang. She wore an evening gown and had a flower in her hair. Gradually couples emerged from the tables and danced, holding each other closely in the half-shadow. The woman's voice carried the couples along, spoke for them, bent and swayed with them. It was like a ceremony, a convulsive rite between the river and the hill in which everyone's movements answered the woman's shout. For the

29

woman, a Rosalba in olive-green, shouted the song, she rocked with her hands on her breasts and shouted; she was invoking something.

Now our Rosalba pressed Poli's hand with rapture and he, quite indifferent, talked with Pieretto.

"The dancers should all be singing themselves," Pieretto said. "There are certain things which ought to be done by ourselves, ourselves alone."

And Poli replied laughing: "When you're dancing, you're already busy. You'll have to excuse them."

"People who dance are stupid," Pieretto replied. "They're looking round for something they've already got in their arms."

Rosalba clapped her hands with the convulsive joy of a child. Those bright eyes of hers disturbed you. The liqueurs and the coffee arrived at that point, and she had to let go of Poli.

The orchestra began again, but this time without any singing. The other instruments went silent and only the piano continued, performing for a few minutes some acrobatic variations worthy of applause. You had to listen even if you didn't want to. Then the orchestra came in on the piano and smothered it. During the number, the lamps and reflectors which illuminated the trees, magically changed colour, and we became green, became red, became yellow.

"Not a bad place," Poli said, looking round.

"Rather dead, these people," Pieretto said. "We ought to have Oreste's scream to wake them up."

Poli raised his head, his eyes surprised, and then remembered. "Our friend's gone to bed?" he enquired immediately. "I wish he were here."

"He's sleeping off last night," Pieretto said. "Pity. He can stand only a certain amount. . . ."

Rosalba made a movement which revealed her to me as though she were naked. She gave a jump. "I want to dance," she said to Poli, annoyed.

"Dear Rosi," he said, "I can't leave my friends alone to be bored. It would be discourteous. We're in Turin, a respectable city."

Rosalba reddened like a flame. I saw then that she was both crazy and awkward. Who knows, perhaps she even had children at Milan. Remembering the story of the flowers she sent to Poli, I stopped looking at her. I heard Pieretto say: "I should be happy to dance with you, Rosalba, but I know I can't aspire to that. I'm not Poli, unfortunately." She gave him a glance that was bewildered rather than angry.

Meanwhile, the orchestra played and I too muttered something. I didn't know how to dance. Poli, impassive, waited for me to finish and then took up:

"I should like you all to know that these days are very important for me. Yesterday I understood many things. That cry the other night has woken me up. It was like the shout that wakens a sleepwalker. It was a sign, the violent crisis that decides an illness. . . ."

"Were you ill?" Rosalba asked.

"I was worse," Poli replied. "I was an old man who thought himself a boy. Now I know that I am a man, a man full of vices, a weak man, but a man. That cry revealed me to myself. I have no illusions about myself."

31

"Power of a cry," Pieretto said.

Without wanting to, I looked closely at Poli's eyes to see if they were clouded.

"I saw my life," Poli continued, "as though it were the life of someone else. I know what I am now, where I come from and what I am doing——"

I interrupted: "But had you ever heard that cry before?"

"You're dense," Pieretto said.

"It was a hunting-call we used to use," Poli said smiling.

"You were hunting!" Rosalba burst out.

"We were on the hill."

An embarrassed silence followed in which everyone except Poli looked at his fingernails. Again the woman was singing in the circle of tables. I heard Rosalba agitatedly beat time with her heel. To the accompaniment of the cadenced voice and the rustling of the couples on the floor, I thought of the chorus of crickets on the black hill.

"Well," Rosalba said at length, "have you any more stories? Do you want to dance now?"

Poli didn't bat an eyelash and didn't move. He was thinking of Oreste's hunting-cry.

"It's beautiful to wake up and have no more illusions," he continued, smiling. "You feel yourself free but responsible. There is a tremendous power within us, freedom. You can reach innocence. You become disposed to suffer."

Rosalba crushed out her cigarette in the saucer. As long as she was quiet, poor thing, so thin and devoured, she was bearable. At least to us who didn't know then what surfeit could mean. Poli's cultured voice calmed her, dominated her. Rosalba twisted about, as though naked.

Finally she leaned close to his face and said: "Tell us straight out what you're thinking. Do you want to get out of Turin?"

His forehead wrinkled, Poli touched her shoulder and took her by the armpit as though he were supporting someone who was falling down. Pieretto leaned forward, almost as though he did not want to miss the scene, and nodded encouragement. Rosalba panted, her eyes half-closed.

"Shall I humour her?" Poli asked us, doubtfully. "Shall I dance with her?"

When the two of us remained alone at the table, Pieretto caught my glance and smiled sarcastically. The voice of the woman in olive filled the night. I scowled and said: "Shit."

Pieretto, who was in good spirits, poured out some liqueur. He poured out a glass for me, and then took more for himself.

"It's like that wherever you go," he declared. "Don't you like them?"

"I said shit."

"Well, the kid's not so very bright," Pieretto said. "There's no limit to what you could do with that woman."

"She's stupid," I said.

"A woman in love is always stupid," Pieretto said.

I listened to some of the words of the song, which guided the couples. They said "Live Live—Take Take"—without passion. However discontented and bored you were, it was

B

difficult to resist the rhythm of the song. I wondered if you could hear the voice from the hill.

"These modern nights," Pieretto said. "They are as old as the world."

5

That night Pieretto danced too, because Rosalba defied Poli and was trying to humiliate him. I don't know how much liqueur we all drank, it seemed that the night would never end. But the orchestra had stopped for some time, and Rosalba called a waiter and wanted Poli to pay the bill and take us all to breakfast in Valentino. I saw the pink gown move in the circle of light under the lampshade—the last one still lit—and cold gusts of nocturnal wind rose out of the Po. But since Poli had turned stubborn and had launched into further conversation with Pieretto and the waiter, Rosalba ran off to the car and began to blow the horn. Then the proprietor, the waiters and the last customers drinking at the bar came out; Rosalba jumped to the ground and called, "Poli! Poli!"

On the way back, Poli drove with one arm round Rosalba and she stretched out, happy, satisfied with him. From time to time she turned round and smiled, as if to encourage us, almost as though we were her accomplices. Pieretto kept quiet all the time. The car didn't turn off towards Turin, but ran over the bridges and burst onto the Moncalieri road. We didn't even stop there: obviously we were riding just to ride, to see the day begin. I closed my eyes, drunk.

A heavy shock awoke me, a tremor as on the edge of a vortex; the nightmare continued for a bit, and a deep, luminous sky opened above me and I seemed to fall head first into it. I woke up in a cold, pink light, the car was bouncing over the cobbles of a small town, it was dawn. Blinking my eyes against the air that rushed by, I saw that Rosalba and Pieretto were sleeping and the town was shuttered up and deserted. Poli managed the wheel, calmly.

He stopped when the sun appeared on the crest of a hill. Pieretto was happy; Rosalba blinked her eyes. My God! she looked pretty old in that low-cut, pink gown. They all made me angry and sorry at the same time; Poli turned round jovially and said good morning.

"It's my fault. Where are we?" I said then.

"Telephone them," Pieretto said. "Tell them that you were sick."

The other two had begun to play about, biting each other's ears. Rosalba took the flower out of her hair, and holding it away from Poli, handed it to me: "There," she said hoarsely. "Don't spoil the party."

As long as the drive lasted I smelled that flower, and it faded. It was the first flower that a woman had given me. and it had to come from someone like Rosalba. I was angry with Poli after his promises the night before.

The bell tower of another village pointed upward. We came into the square through a porticoed street, under rounded, protruding balconies, and in the shade of the morning a girl sprinkled water from a bottle onto the cobbles

The wooden floor of the café had also been sprinkled and smelled cellarish and rainy. We sat down at a window with our backs to the sun, and I immediately asked for the telephone. There wasn't any.

"It's your fault," Poli said to Rosalba. "If you hadn't made me dance——"

36

"If you hadn't been drinking," she snapped. "You got to the point where you couldn't understand anything any more. You were sweating cognac."

"Drop it," Poli said.

"Ask your friends the things you said," she shouted disgustedly. "Ask them! They heard."

Pieretto said: "Important matters. All about Innocence and Free Choice."

The woman who served us and looked curiously at Rosalba told me that there was a telephone at the post office. Then I pushed back my chair to get up and asked Pieretto for his wallet. Rosalba got up too and said: "I'm coming with you. It'll wake me up. It's like a madhouse in here."

And so the two of us went out into the square, she in pink, tall and thin, a sight. Heads were leaning out of the windows, but the street was still empty.

"They're all in the fields at this hour," I said in order to say something.

Rosalba asked me for a cigarette.

"Ordinary Macedonias," I said.

She stopped so that I could light her cigarette and when we were face to face she said with a low, forced laugh: "You're younger than Poli."

I snapped away the match which was burning my fingers.

Rosalba continued, warming up: "More sincere than Poli."

I drew back a bit, but continued to look at her.

"Well, let's get it over with," she said. "It's my neck, don't pay any attention. . . . Now tell me something."

She asked hoarsely what we had been doing these days

37

when we were with Poli. When I began with the meeting, she blinked her eyes. "Poli was alone?" she wanted to know. "But then why should he have been on the hill at midnight?"

"He was alone, but it was three o'clock, not midnight."

"And how did you happen to be with him that night?"

I told her that Oreste and Pieretto knew Poli better than I. Oreste and I had gone to bed, but Pieretto had been with him the whole evening. Poli had seemed a bit drunk. That is, he seemed more or less as usual. I told her that she should ask Pieretto, for the two of them had talked together a good deal.

Instantly I realized that Rosalba had lost no time and had already interrogated Pieretto while they were dancing. She stared at me. Annoyed, I drew away and we continued on our way over the cobbles.

While awaiting my turn in the post office, Rosalba smoked in the doorway; I turned to her and said: "Oreste has known Poli ever since he was a boy. . . . He was with us the other night."

She didn't answer and looked out into the street. I came to the door too and examined the sky.

I went into the small booth and spoke to my mother. When I came out and turned to the door, Rosalba had not moved. I said lightheartedly: "Shall we go?"

"Your friend," she began again, trembling, "he's a very clever chap. . . . Didn't he mention anything that Poli had told him?"

"They went up to the lakes."

"I know that."

"He was drunk and got sick."

"No, before that," Rosalba said impatiently, and her voice trembled.

"I don't know. We found him on the hill looking at the stars."

Then with a wriggle, Rosalba took my arm. Two peasants who were passing by turned round to look at us. "You understand me, don't you?" Rosalba said, breathing hard. "You've seen how Poli treats me. Yesterday I thought I'd die. I've been alone in the hotel for three days. I don't dare go out and take a walk because everyone knows me. I'm in his hands here; at Milan they think I've gone to the seaside. But Poli doesn't pay any attention to me, Poli is tired of me, he doesn't even want to dance with me. . . ."

I looked at the cobbles and imagined the heads looking down from the balconies.

". . . you saw him in a good mood tonight. When he's drunk he can still stand me; but he gets drunk, and worse, just so that he can forget how distasteful I am to him. Now. . . ." here her voice became more troubled, "we live just from one day to the next."

She didn't free my arm even when I raised the tinkling chain curtain so that we could enter the café. Poli and Pieretto were talking away in the shadow and Pieretto shouted: "What are we going to have to eat?"

Fried eggs and cherries were placed before us. I tried not to look at Rosalba. Poli continued his talk, breaking off a piece of bread.

"The more you decide, the more you fall down. You touch bottom. Then, when everything is lost, you discover yourself."

Pieretto laughed. "A drunk is a drunk," he said. "Man no

longer has a choice in the matter of drugs or wine. He chose once and for all, millions of years ago, when he shouted the first *evoe*."

"There's an innocence," Poli said, "a clarity which comes up from the deeps——"

Rosalba kept silent, I didn't dare look at her.

"I tell you," Pieretto interrupted, "that when you forgot what time it was last night, it was because you had lost any choice in the matter."

"But I . . . I'm the one who's trying to . . . to find this innocence," Poli said, faltering but going on doggedly. "The oftener I recognize it the more I am convinced that I am base and a man. Do you or don't you believe that man's state is weakness? . . . . How can you rise up if you haven't first fallen headlong?"

Rosalba nibbled at cherries and kept silent. Pieretto shook his head several times and said: "No." I thought about my conversation with Rosalba and not so much about the words as about her voice and how she had gripped my arm. My eyes burned from tiredness. When we got up to leave, I glanced at her. She seemed to me calm, half-asleep.

6

We left them at the door of their hotel in the squalor of a wasted morning. The sun beating on the shop windows hurt my eyes. I crossed through the gardens with Pieretto and we didn't speak; I thought about Oreste.

"Be seeing you," I said at the corner.

I went home and dropped into bed. I heard my mother moving about in the hallway and I postponed the moment when we would meet. I didn't want to sleep, only to pull myself together. Being so tired, I found it easy not to think about the night, all the confusion and Rosalba's sobbing; and I fell into that sky I had dreamed about while dozing in the car under the cool light, I lingered in the streets of the village, as I looked up. I was well acquainted with such villages grouped together in the country. There was the summer vegetable garden beside my grandparents' house, where father and mother used to send me to spend my summers when I was a boy. The village, standing in the plain between irrigation channels and hedgerows, had porticoed streets and you had to look up to see slices of sky. All that remained of my infancy were those summers. The narrow streets which led into the fields on every side, during the day and in the evening, were gateways to life and the world. It was a great marvel when a motor car, coming from God knows where, honked its way through the main street of the town and went on, God knows where, to new

41

cities, towards the sea, scattering the children and dust in confusion.

In the dark, I recalled the project of hiking over the hills with Pieretto, our knapsacks on our shoulders. I did not envy the motor cars. I knew that in a car you cross over but do not come to know a land. 'On foot,' I imagined myself saying to Pieretto, 'that's the real way to get about in the country, you take the paths, you pass by the vineyards, you see everything. It's the same difference as looking at water or jumping in. Better to be a beggar, a vagabond.'

Pieretto laughed out of the dark and told me that petrol covers the whole world.

'The devil,' I muttered. 'Peasants don't know what petrol is. Sickles and mattocks, that's what's important to them. Before washing out a cask or cutting down a tree they still study the moon. I've seen them. When hail threatens, they stretch two chains out on the threshing floor. . . .'

'And they buy insurance policies,' Pieretto said. 'And they use threshing machines. And they spray Bordeaux mixture on the vines.'

'They make use of these things,' I cried in a low voice. 'The peasants make use of them, but they live differently. They're uncomfortable in the city.'

Pieretto laughed harshly. 'Give a peasant a car,' he smiled ironically. 'You'll soon see how he speeds along. You can bet he wouldn't stop to give either Rosalba or us a lift. A peasant is a business man.'

I thought of Oreste who was studying to be a doctor. 'There you have a peasant who lives in the city,' I said to

Pieretto. 'He's more scientific than we are, but the old life dies hard. For him night means something different from what it means to us, as you yourself say——'

The telephone bell interrupted my dozing dream. My parents called me. I thought that it was Rosalba, that the story hadn't finished yet. But it was Pieretto's sister, she wanted to know whether I had seen him—he hadn't been home for two days. "I left him half an hour ago," I told her. "He was on his way home." In order not to cause any trouble, I said nothing about the night.

She said: "What a bunch you are! Where did you sleep?"

"We didn't sleep."

"When you sleep you can't get into trouble," she said laughing.

"And who feels like sleeping?"

At table I said that we had had a puncture. My father said that a blown tyre can cause an accident, especially if the driver has been drinking. Then he said that you shouldn't take advantage of your friends: that you can never get out of debt to one who has considerable means.

In the afternoon I decided to study. But first I took a bath in order to refresh myself. I thought that Rosalba and Poli were probably bathing too, and I wondered if Rosalba wasn't too old to undress. Towards evening the telephone rang. It was Pieretto. "Come to Oreste's," he said immediately.

"But suppose I'm studying?"

"Come along anyhow; it's interesting," he said. "That pair . . . . There's been a shooting."

We sweated in the restaurant talking with Oreste, who had come from the hospital and then had telephoned the nurses twice to get news. Poli was dying; the bullet had entered his side and grazed a lung; and Rosalba had been shouting to the waiters who were running about: "Kill me! Kill me! Why don't you kill me!" Finally they had had to shut her up in the bathroom.

"When did it happen?" I asked.

Oreste said: "She shot him in a fit of anger. She had been screaming before then, and the people could hear her all the way downstairs in the bar. I wonder what sort of filthy thing's behind it all? . . . ."

It had happened half-way through the afternoon, in the heat of the day. Poli must have taken dope before anything had happened, for he was laughing in the hospital cot, quite gay.

We discussed it all evening. Now the people at the hospital and at the hotel were waiting for instructions from Milan. Rosalba was shut up in the room; her fate depended on Poli's life and on the arrival of his father: he was a man who, hating scandal, could stop any inquest with two words and silence everything and everyone. There was, of course, Rosalba's revolver, a woman's plaything with a mother-of-pearl grip, but someone was ready to substitute another weapon for it.

"Power of money," Pieretto said, impassively. "You can even pay for a crime or an agony."

Oreste telephoned again. "The old man's coming," he said, turning to us. "It's a good thing. I wonder if he knows the woman? . . . ."

Then we told him that Poli was really the guilty one, that we had spent the night with them and that Poli had treated her like an utter rotter. "He was asking for it," Pieretto said. "And a Rosalba like that was made to do it."

"I'm going back to the hospital immediately," Oreste said. "They're giving him a transfusion."

That night I took a walk with Pieretto. I was worn out by excitement and lack of sleep, and he pondered, voicing his opinions. I confided that Rosalba had asked me about Poli.

"It was obvious that something had to happen," Pieretto said. "A woman can take everything from a man, except a crisis of conscience. Do you know what she told me last night? That young as he is, Poli no longer turns round to look at women who pass by in the street or in hotel corridors."

"She asked me what we were doing on the hill."

"She would have preferred him to have done something swinish. You know. . . . A woman can understand that sort of thing better."

Then I said that as far as I was concerned he *was* a swine. Coke or free choice—they both seemed to me to be bestialities. He poked fun at people, mocked them, that's what he did. And it was a good thing he had been shot.

Pieretto smiled and said that whether Poli lived or died, we had had a fine experience. "You don't think so, though," he said. "What do we look for every evening when we wander about the streets? Something to break the monotony, to vary the day. . . ."

45

"I'd like to know how you'd feel if it had happened to you."

"What! . . . And night and day you're thinking about how to get out of the squirrel-cage. Why do you suppose we go beyond the Po? . . . . Only you're mistaken: the most unforeseen things happen in a room in Turin, in a café, on a tram. . . ."

"I'm not looking for unforeseen things."

"Well," he said. "This world is made for the Poli's. Believe me."

The next day Poli was still hovering between life and death; and they gave him another transfusion and he sweated in the cot. According to Oreste, who alternated with the father in sitting by Poli's bedside, the drug had worn off and Poli resembled a frightened baby about to cry. The old man had immediately gone to Rosalba that night; he, Oreste, didn't know what had been said; but Rosalba had been shut up in a pension run by nuns, arĩd no one mentioned homicide any more. "An accident," the chief surgeon said, speaking to his assistants. This was the sort of news that Pieretto liked to hear, and Oreste knew it.

Poor Oreste, he was nearly on the point of missing his exams. He took his turns at Poli's pillow like a nurse. He spoke with the old *commendatore* and introduced himself. He said that the old man talked about the country, about the Coste and the harvests as one who understands such things. He arrived at the hospital driving Poli's green car. It was he who sent Oreste to bed in the morning.

Finally the news came that Poli had recovered. Pieretto

also went to visit him. He said: "He's just the same as ever and is reading Nino Salvaneschi." I resolved not to go. We talked about it for a few more days, then Oreste told us that he had been sent to the seaside in an auto-ambulance.

7

That summer I spent an hour or two at the river every morning. It was pleasant to sweat at the oars and then dive into the cold, dark water, keeping my eyes open and letting the water refresh them. Most of the time I went alone, for Pieretto would be sleeping at that hour. When he came along, he would handle the boat while I swam. We used to row up against the current under the bridges, along the walled banks, and come out between the embankment and trees under the hillside. Towering over us, the hill was beautiful as we drifted back, smoking the first pipeful; and, though June, at that hour it was still veiled in dampness and exhaled a fresh breath of roots. Seated on the thwarts of that boat I developed a taste for the open air and came to understand that the pleasure we get from water and earth is something that continues from the far side of infancy, from the far side of a vegetable garden and an orchard. Those mornings I used to think that all life is like a game beneath the sun.

But the sanddiggers who stood in the water up to their thighs were not playing any game; they hoisted shovelfuls of sludge and emptied them into the barge, breathing hard. After an hour or two hours, the barge would glide down the river, heaped high, and a thin, blackened man with a waistcoat over his naked torso manœuvred it slowly with a pole. He unloaded his sand in the city, below the bridges, and returned slowly; they would come up in groups beneath a sun reaching the zenith. By the time I left the river, they would have made two or three trips. All day while I wandered about in the city, while I studied, talked or rested, they went up and down the river, unloading, jumping into the water, broiling in the sun. I used to think about them especially towards evening when our nocturnal life would begin and they would go home to the huts along the river in the low-lying popular sections and throw themselves down to sleep. Or perhaps they would drain off a glass of wine at the inn. Certainly they too knew the sun and the hill well.

Whenever I spent the noon sweating in the boat, then the rest of the day my blood would stay fresh, invigorated by my plunge into the river. It was as if the sun and the living weight of the current had imbued in me a virtue of theirs, a blind force, joyous and stubborn, like that of a tree trunk or a woodland beast. When Pieretto came with me, he too would enjoy the morning. Drifting down towards Turin on the current, eyes washed by the sun and the water, we would lie flat in the boat and let ourselves dry in the sun, and the banks, the hill, the villas, the forms of distant trees were incised in the air.

"If you lived this sort of life every day," Pieretto said, "you'd become an animal."

"You only have to look at the sanddiggers. . . ."

"No, not them," he said, "they just work. . . . You'd become an animal of health and strength. . . . And of egoism," he added immediately, "of that mild egoism of a person growing fat."

"There's nothing wrong with that," I shouted.

"Who said there was? Being born is nobody's fault. It's

the fault of others, always of others. All we do is go boating
and smoke our pipes."

"We're not sufficiently animal."

Pieretto laughed. "Who knows what a real animal is?"
he said. "A fish, a blackbird, a lizard? . . . . Or even a
squirrel? . . . . Some say that inside every animal is a soul
. . . a soul in torment. That would be purgatory. . . ."

"Nothing," he continued, "has the smell of death about
it as much as the sun in summer, the strong light, exuberant
nature. You sniff the air and you smell the woods, and you
realise that the plants and animals don't give a damn
about you. Everything lives and consumes itself. Nature is
death. . . ."

"What's purgatory have to do with it?" I asked.

"There's no other way to explain it," he said. "Either
there is nothing, or the souls are there."

It was an old argument. That was what irritated me in
Pieretto. I'm not like Oreste who at these retorts would
merely shrug his shoulders and laugh. Every word with a
savour of the country touches and excites me. I didn't
manage to answer him then, and I kept silent and rowed.

Pieretto, too, drank in the sparkling water with his eyes.
The year before it was he who had said: "But there's the
Po. . . . Why shouldn't we go there?" And so had con-
quered our timidity, mine and Oreste's, for we wouldn't do
certain things merely because we had never done them
before. Pieretto had been in Turin only a few years, and
previously he had lived in different cities, accompanying his
father, a restless architect who rooted and uprooted his
family capriciously. Once, when he was directing the restora-
tion of a convent in Puglia, he had settled his wife and

50

daughters with the nuns while he and Pieretto lived in a cell with monks. "My father," Pieretto said once, "doesn't know what to say to priests. They give him the shivers. He can't stand them and he used to fight with us because he was terrified lest I become a priest or monk." Now his father, a giant of a man who wore his shirt open at the neck, had calmed down and was happy in Turin; he kept his family there while he travelled about; the few times that I had seen him, he and his son had made fun of one another, given one another advice, talked as I didn't know a son could talk with his father. At bottom I didn't like such too-free ways, and his father seemed to me an ineffectual contemporary of ours.

"You were well off in the convent," Pieretto once said to him, "because you lived the life of a batchelor."

"Rubbish," the old man said. "You're well off wherever your soul is in peace. See how the monks get fat."

"There are thin ones too."

"They're monks by mistake, sad people. It's a bad sign, being a saint. It means you can't live with others."

"Like travelling on a motorbike," Pieretto said. "It's like a monk riding a motorbike. Who can seriously believe in him?"

The old man looked at him suspiciously.

"What's so bad about that?"

"Nothing," Pieretto said. "Nowadays a saint is like a monk riding a motorbike. . . ."

"An anachronism," I said.

"Business," the old man said, irritated. "Religion is all business, all commercialism. They know that better than we do."

The Devil in the Hills

That year the old man was working at Genoa where he had a contract, and Pieretto had to go there for the sea-bathing. His sister left about that time, and Pieretto wanted us to go there too so that we might see a bit of life. But there was that other project of going to Oreste's: for me, too many is too much, and the Po was my excuse not to go to the seaside. I decided to remain alone in Turin and wait for the two of them to return and then we would shoulder our knapsacks and be off.

I would never have believed that spending the beginning of the summer in the city could have been so pleasant. Without a friend or a familiar face in the streets, I thought over the past days, went boating, imagined new things. My most restless hours were during the night—of course, Pieretto had debauched me; the most beautiful were midday towards two o'clock when the empty streets contained only a slice of sky. Often I would notice some woman at her window, bored and absorbed as only women know how to be, and I would raise my head in passing, catch sight of an interior, a room, a sliver of mirror; and I would carry that delight away with me. I wasn't envious of my two friends who spent those hours at the beach, in cafés, among tanned and half-naked girls. Of course they were having a good time, but they would come back; and meantime I spent my mornings tanning myself; sweating and enjoying my lot. Girls came to the Po too, they screamed from the boats and the banks of the Sangone; even the sanddiggers raised their caps and spoke to them; I knew that some day I should meet one of them, something would happen. I pictured the eyes, legs and shoulders of a striking woman, really stupendous, and continued to row and smoke my pipe. It was difficult, standing up in the boat and pushing on the oars, not to assume the posture of an athletic and primitive man, not to peer at the horizon or the hill. I wondered if people like Poli would have enjoyed my pleasures and understood my life.

Towards the end of July I took a girl to the Po, but she was nothing striking or novel. I already knew her, she was a shop girl in a book store, strong and nearsighted, but she had well-kept hands and a languid manner, and while I was browsing among the books she asked me where had I got so tanned. She promised happily to come that Saturday.

She wore a brief white bathing-suit under her skirt, which she removed after laughingly turning her back to me. She stretched out on the cushions in the bottom of the boat saying that the sun was hot and watched me row. Her name was Teresina-Resina. We exchanged some words about the heat, the fishermen, the bathing establishments at Moncalieri. She talked about swimming pools rather than the river. She asked me if I often danced. With her eyes half-closed, she seemed distracted.

I landed the boat under the trees and began to swim. She didn't come in because she had covered herself with sun tan oil; there was an odour of cosmetics about her. When I came dripping out of the water, she said that I was a good swimmer; and she walked up and down along the bank. Her long, reddened legs were'nt bad at all. I don't know why, but I felt sorry for her. I arranged some cushions on the stones and she handed me the sun tan oil and asked me to oil her back where she couldn't reach. Then kneeling down behind her I rubbed her back with my fingers and she laughed and told me to be good, she laughed leaning back against me so that the nape of her neck touched my mouth. Turning round she kissed me on the mouth. She knew what she was doing. I said: "Why did you have to go and rub yourself with that oil?"

And Resina, touching her nose to mine, said: "Why, sir! you cad, sir! What are you thinking of? . . . It's no go."

Her small eyes continued to laugh and she asked me why I didn't grease myself too. Then I pressed her to me. She wriggled out of my arms and said: "No, no. Rub yourself with the oil."

She wouldn't do anything more than kiss, even though she agreed to come into the bushes with me. After the initial annoyance was over, I wasn't sorry that things had ended like that. On the grass under the sun, our bodies and the odour of the sun tan oil were out of tune; it is something to do in the city, in a room. A naked body is not beautiful in the open air. The idea bothered me; it offended those places. Then I took her to one of the bathing establishments where there was a swimming pool, and Resina, contented, watched the other girls and drank a bottle of cream soda through a straw.

8

I didn't show up again at Resina's shop because the sun
tan oil, the swimming pool and the implicit contract of the
game annoyed me. All in all, I was better off alone, and
she wasn't the first who had disappointed me. Which means
that instead of being able to brag to Pieretto about a great
conquest I would say that no woman is worth a morning
of sun and water. I already knew what he would reply: "A
morning, probably. not; but a night, certainly."

I somehow couldn't picture Oreste at the seaside with
Pieretto. The year before, when I had gone with Pieretto
and his sister, Oreste hadn't come. He had immediately gone
to his village in the hills. "What can he find to do there?"
Pieretto had asked. "We'll have to go too." That was how
the project of going on foot was born; but during the winter
Oreste had advised us against it, saying that it was better
to spend a month among the vineyards than on the roads.
He was not wrong, but Pieretto said no. Pieretto was not
the sort to keep still, and when I had been with him the
year before, he had looked for a new beach every morning,
nosed about everywhere, made friends from one end of the
coast to the other—in wineshops or big hotels, he had no
preferences. Knowing no dialects, he spoke them all. He
would say, "This evening at the Casino"—and it might be
addressed to a vacationer or the proprietor of some shop or
an old lady who rented apartments; he would locate the
point of least resistance and spend the evening at the

casino. It made you laugh to watch him. But he had no success with women. His manner was useless with them. He overwhelmed and drowned them with words; then he would lose patience and insult them; the move would fail. I wasn't even sure that he wanted to succeed. "You've got to be stupid," I would console him, "in order to get anywhere with women."

"That's not true," he replied. "That's not enough. You have to be stupid *too*." Pieretto was short and curly-haired, dark-skinned with dry cheeks; he seemed born to steal a girl from anyone just by laughing or looking at her. Compared with myself or with Oreste, who was big and strong, there was no doubt who was most outstanding. And yet even at the seaside Pieretto managed nothing. "You're too fast," I told him. "You don't let them get to know you. A girl likes to know the sort of chap she's dealing with."

We walked along the coast road above the sheer rock shelving, looking for a certain beach.

"Here are the women and here's the beach," he said.

Down below, small in the distance, Linda and Carlotta were undressing—his sister and a friend of hers, a well-built girl older than us: had we seen them walking by on the street we would have turned round to look at them.

"Pleasant thought," he said; "they're waiting for us."

"Linda brought her for you."

Pieretto raised his hand in the strong sunlight and gave a shout. But the noise of the sea which scarcely reached to where we were must have drowned his voice. Then we threw some stones. The girls raised their heads and waved. They must have shouted something but we didn't hear.

"Let's go down," I said.

We got to the beach swimming across the green water of a small inlet. We flirted with the girls for a long time on the rocks and in the spray. Then stretching out under the weight of the sun, I watched the froth which ran along the sand, and Pieretto talked with his sister and her friend. I remember that we ate peaches.

They were talking about the fruit-stones and the scraps of newspaper that you find even on deserted beaches. Pieretto said that there were no more virgin spots in the world. He said that the clouds and sea horizon still have an untouched, untamed air for many people. He said that man's old pretension to finding his woman intact was a residue of that same taste—the insane mania for being first. Carlotta, her hair in her eyes, argued with him: she didn't understand that he was joking, and laughed resentfully.

That he should have talked that way with her of all people! Carlotta was the sort who said simply, "Oh, how lovely!"—whether of the sea, of a baby or of a cat. She had, of course, various boy friends at the beach and at dances, but she maintained that she just couldn't keep company in the city with boys who had seen her half-naked on the beach. She and Linda used to take walks together, arm in arm.

Pieretto paid no attention to these things. From the rock on which she was lying, Linda shouted to him to leave off it. Pieretto began to talk about blood. He said that a taste for the intact and untamed was basically a taste for shedding blood. "You make love in order to wound, to shed blood," he explained. "The *bourgeois* who marries and hopes to have a virgin bride wants to sate his desire. . . ."

"Oh, shut up!" Carlotta shouted.

"Why?" he said. "We all hope we'll have our chance. . . ."

Linda got up, stretched in the sun and suggested that we swim.

"People go mountaineering and hunting for the same reason," Pieretto said. "Solitude in the country arouses the thirst for blood. . . ."

After that day, beautiful Carlotta wasn't seen any more on intact beaches. Linda said to us: "You mean you really expected to see her again?" That was the way Pieretto handled girls, and he would maintain that he had manœuvred well and had held the advantage. Then he would discover new places and new people and the conversation would change. When the vacation was over, he had no close friendships, except perhaps among some owners of wine-shops or some old pensioners.

I thought back upon that hidden beach for a long time. But, at the bottom, the wide, untrammelled sea meant little to me; I liked confined places, which thereby had form and meaning—inlets, narrow streets, terraces, olive yards. At times, flat on a rock, I would scrutinize a piece of stone a few inches from my eyes and no bigger than my fist; against the sky it would resemble a huge mountain. That is the sort of thing I like.

Now I thought about Oreste, who was seeing the sea for the first time. Pieretto wouldn't have let him sleep and I knew that they were capable of anything together, from nude bathing to visiting the town's seven churches. Then there was Linda and her friends, there was his father, a violent and unpredictable person. I sometimes did miss our occasionally getting up before dawn to walk unseen along the sea in the heat of the last stars. I knew that Oreste would have no need of titillations to enjoy his vacation. But I would have paid a lot to hear him tell me, as I rowed him on the Po, exactly what he thought of that Riviera world.

But neither he nor Pieretto returned to Turin. Linda, who worked in an office, came back and telephoned me about the first of August. "Listen," she said, "Pieretto and Oreste are waiting for you in some village. I don't remember the name. Come round and I'll give you the instructions." I mentioned a name at once, Oreste's hills. That was it. Those rotters had already gone.

I met her before dinner in front of the café she usually frequented. She was so tanned that I scarcely recognized her. She talked and laughed with me vivaciously, in the manner in which boys and girls flirt. "Buy me a vermouth?" she asked. "It's an old seaside custom."

She sat down, crossing her legs. "It's awful coming back in August," she sighed. "Lucky you; you stayed put."

We talked about the other two. "I have no idea what they did," she said. "I left them strictly alone; they're old enough. This year I had my own friends, grown-ups—too grown up for you kids. . . ."

"And Carlotta? Beautiful Carlotta?"

Linda threw open her mouth and laughed. "Pieretto sometimes goes too far. Everybody in the family is like that. I am too. We're pretty bad. And we get worse every year."

I didn't say no and studied her closely. She became aware of my examination and made a face at me.

"I'll never see twenty again," she murmured. "But I'm not too old either."

"People who are old are born old," I said; "no one grows old."

"That's the sort of remark Pieretto makes," Linda cried. "It's an authentic Pieretto."

I made a face too. "We'll make up one a day," I said, "until we've had enough."

9

Oreste's house had a peeling, reddish terrace, and it overlooked a sea of valleys and ravines bathed in a strong light which hurt your eyes. All morning I had ridden through the plain, a plain which looked familiar to me, and looking out of the train window I had caught sight of hedgerows, mirrors of water, flocks of geese and meadow expanses that I recognized from my infancy. I was still thinking about these things when we entered between precipitous banks and you had to look up to see the sky. The train stopped beyond a narrow tunnel. I found myself in the heat and dust of the station square, my eyes meeting chalky slopes on all sides. A fat waggon-driver showed me the road; I had a good way to climb, for the village was high up. I threw my bag on the waggon and we went up together, matching the slow pace of the oxen.

To reach the top we passed by vineyards and scorched stubble; and as the slope levelled off beneath my feet, I distinguished new villages, new vineyards, new hillsides. I asked the waggon-driver where all the vines had come from and whether there were enough farmhands to cultivate them. He looked at me curiously; he talked volubly and tried to find out who I was. He said: "There have always been vines. It's not like building a house, you know."

When we were under the great wall that shored up the village, I was about to ask him whose idea it had been to build houses way up there, but the narrowed eyes set in his dark face kept me silent. I breathed an odour of mingled wind and figs which, there on the slope, reminded me of the seaside. I drew a breath and murmured: "How fresh the air is!"

The town was a stony street on which courtyards and balconies opened. I saw a garden full of dahlias, zinnias and geraniums—scarlet and yellow predominating—and bean and squash flowers. Between one house and another there were cool corners, stairways, chicken coops and old peasant women. Oreste's house was at the corner of the square, on the terrace formed by the great retaining wall; it was reddish and stained—a villa discoloured by creepers and the wind. For the wind blew up there even before noon: I had noticed it as soon as I had come into the square and the waggon-driver had shown me the house. I was sweaty and I went straight up the three steps to the door. I hammered with the bronze knocker.

While I waited, I looked about at the paint peeling in the sunlight, the clumps of weeds on the terrace against the sky, the great midday silence. And as the creaking of the cart diminished in the distance, I thought of how these things were all familiar to Oreste; he had been born and had grown up here; they must all have had some special meaning for him. I thought of how many places in the world belong to other people in the same way, places that they have in their blood and that no one else knows. I touched the door with my hand.

Through half-closed shutters, a woman replied to my knocking. She shouted and asked me questions. Neither Oreste nor Pieretto was at home. She told me to wait a moment; I begged pardon for having arrived at such an hour. Finally the door opened.

Females appeared everywhere—old women, little girls, babies. Oreste's mother, a large woman wearing a kitchen apron, welcomed me excitedly, asked about my trip and showed me into a darkened room—after the shutters were opened, I noticed demitasses, paintings, covered furniture, a bamboo tripod and vases of flowers. She asked if I would like a cup of coffee. There was a close odour of bread and fruit. She sat down and talked with me, Oreste's superior smile on her lips. She told me that Oreste would be back immediately, that all the men would be back and we would eat in an hour, that all Oreste's friends were fine boys— didn't we go to the same school? Then she got up and said, "There's a wind," and closed the shutters. "You'll have to excuse us; you'll all have to sleep in the same room. . . . Would you like to freshen up?"

When Oreste and Pieretto arrived I already knew the whole house. Our room gave on the distant hills, and you washed in a basin, spattering water on the red tiles. "Don't worry if you splash water on the floor," his mother had said. "It chases the flies away." I had gone out on the terrace and descended into the kitchen, where the women worked over the crackling brushwood in the fireplace. I had leafed through almanacks and old schoolbooks in the father's office, which he later entered talking loudly; I recognized him at once from the photographs in the living-room. He wore a moustache and he lit my cigarette and talked to me about many things. He wanted to know if I had come from the seaside too, if my father had any farm property, if I had studied to be a priest as my friend had. I felt my way cautiously, letting him talk first. After all, even that was possible.

"Did Oreste tell you that?"

"You know how it is," he said, "we talk a lot. The women believe in these things. . . . They want to believe in them . . . . This chap Pieretto knows a good deal about priests: he's studied and can tell you all about the seminary and the rules. . . . My sister-in-law wants to speak to the dean about him."

"He just talks for the sake of talking. Haven't you discovered that yet?"

"As for me," he said, "it's all just commercialism. But the women lose their heads over it."

"That's what his father says." I told him how Pieretto had happened to live in the convent, and explained that he had understood the priests and had seen them work and that neither he nor his father was a believer. "He's just amusing himself, that's all."

"I'm glad," he said. "I'm really glad. For heaven's sake don't say anything about that. In a monastery. . . . Well, what do you know about that? . . . ."

Oreste and Pieretto arrived and clapped me on the back. They were brown and famished, and we went to the table immediately. His father sat at the head of the table; the women came and went, old aunts and little sisters. I met Pieretto's victim, the sister-in-law Giustina, an old ruddy-complexioned lady seated at the other end of the table. The little girls joked and teased her and told about some flowers for the altar which the sacristan had put in the holy water. There was an allusion to the Feast of the Assumption. I watched everyone closely, but Pieretto seemed to have been warned: he ate and kept silent.

Nothing happened. We talked about Oreste's vacation at the seaside. I said that I had been sunbathing on the Po and that the Po was full of bathers. The little girls listened attentively. The father let me finish, then he said that there was sun everywhere, but that in his time only invalids went to the Riviera.

"You don't go for the sun," Pieretto said. "Nor yet for the sea."

"Why do you go then?" Oreste said.

"To see your neighbour as naked as yourself."

"Are there bathing establishments on the Po, too?" the mother asked me hastily.

"Sure thing," Oreste said. "And there's singing and dancing."

"Naked," Pieretto said.

Old Giustina snorted at the foot of the table. "I can understand men going there," she said scornfully. "But it's shameful that young ladies should go. The men ought to go alone."

"You don't mean that men should dance together!" Pieretto said. "That would be indecent."

"It's more indecent for girls to undress in public," the old woman cried.

And so we continued stuffing ourselves greedily, and the conversation turned, hesitated and then ran on. Occasionally it concerned their own matters—village gossip, questions of work and land—but as soon as Pieretto would open his mouth the conversation would grow heated. If we hadn't been staying there all together and his comportment hadn't become mine, I might have enjoyed myself. However, Oreste looked at me happily, with laughing eyes; he was glad to have me in his home. I shook my fist at him and then described a walking movement with two fingers. He didn't understand and glanced round comically. He thought I was bored sitting at table.

"Fine trick," I said to him. "Weren't we supposed to hike here from Turin?"

Oreste shrugged his shoulders. "We'll have plenty of walking up hillsides and through the vineyards," he said. "You'll see. That's what we're here for—to take walks."

His father hadn't understood. We told him that we had planned to hike here from Turin. One of Oreste's little sisters made a surprised sound and clapped her hands over her mouth.

His father said, "But there's a train. . . . What an idea!"

Pieretto intervened. "As soon as everyone starts going by train then it becomes more fun to walk. It's a fashion like sea-bathing. Now that everyone has bathtubs in the home, it's more fun to bathe in public.

"Speak for yourself," I said.

"How strange people are!" the father said. "In my days only women followed fashions."

We got up from the table, sluggish and sleepy. The women hadn't left my plate empty for a moment, and Oreste's father never left off filling my glass with wine. "Go to sleep; it's too hot to do anything," they told me.

The three of us went up to the torrid room. I bathed my face in the white basin in order to revive myself. I said to Oreste: "How long does the holiday last?"

"What holiday?"

"It seems as though we're in the middle of one. You must eat up a vineyard every meal."

Pieretto said: "Imagine if you'd come on foot!"

Laughing, Oreste stood before the half-closed shutters, which threw horizontal shafts of sunlight on his trunk. He had taken off his shirt and you could see his black, bulging muscles. "I feel good," he said and dropped onto the bed.

"Oreste's developed a taste for dancing and feeling the girls," Pieretto said. "You should have seen him dance—he looked as though he was in a high sea. Like Pavlov's dogs: show him a girl now and he smells salt air."

"These fields have a flavour of the sea," I said, putting my head down to the open half of the shutter. "Look down there. It even looks like a sea."

Pieretto said: "Go ahead and get your fill of the panorama. It's all right on your first day. But tomorrow you have to leave off."

I let them laugh and talk a bit. "You seem awfully happy," I said. "What's going on?"

"You've eaten and drunk. What more do you want?" Pieretto said.

Oreste said: "You want to smoke your pipe?"

The tone of conspiracy in the dark room made me ill at ease. I said to Pieretto: "You've already frightened all the women of the house. Same old Pieretto. . . . But in the end they'll throw you out."

Oreste swung up to a sitting position. "No tricks now. You're staying for the vintage."

"What'll we do all August?" I shouted. I pulled my vest

over my head. When I had got out of it, I heard Pieretto say: ". . . Why, he's as brown as a nut."

"There's sun on the Po. The Riviera's not the only place," I shouted, and they began to laugh again.

"What's the matter? Are you both drunk?"

"Let's see your belly-button," Oreste said.

I pushed down my belt, revealing a strip of pallid belly. They hooted and shouted: *"L'infame!* Of course he'd have the mark!"

"You've still got the mark of shame." Pieretto cackled in his spitting way. "You'd better come along to the cleft. No proprieties to observe there. One should hide nothing from the sun."

10

We went the next day. A thin watercourse ran right down the middle of the hollow that divided our hill from the irregular downs, and we descended from the vineyards, among fields of millet, until we came to a steep cleft, full of acacias and alders. At the bottom, the thread of water had formed a string of shallow puddles; there was one below a spring, from which we could see only the sky and the screen of briars. During the hot hours the sun beat straight down into it.

"What a country!" Pieretto said. "You have to go underground to be naked."

For this is what they would do: they would leave home towards noon and then spend an hour or two down there as naked as snakes, sunbathing between the walls of cracked earth. Their aim was to sun their groins and buttocks, to cancel the shame, darken everything. Then they would go to lunch. They were returning from the cleft the day I arrived.

Now I understood the talk and the agitation of the women. They didn't know about Pieretto's discovery, but sunbathing in the midst of fields of millet—even without girls or in shorts—was a striking notion.

That afternoon I discovered other things. The first day you arrive somewhere, it is hard to sleep, even when everybody takes a nap. While the house dozed and flies buzzed everywhere, I descended the stone stairway and went to the kitchen from which issued dull thuds, like the rocking of a cradle, and the sounds of voices. When I opened the door, I found one of the little girls, together with Oreste's mother, who, her sleeves rolled up, vigorously kneaded dough on the cleared table. An old woman was washing dishes in a tub. They smiled and told me that they were preparing dinner.

"So soon?" I exclaimed.

The old woman at the tub turned round with a toothless smile. "It will be ready soon," she croaked.

Oreste's mother dried her forehead and said: "There are too many women in this house. Two men or four men—it doesn't matter, the work is always the same."

The little girl with blonde braids stood watching me with amazement as she emptied water from a ladle onto the flour. "Look sharp, silly!" her mother said, and continued kneading.

I remained watching. I said I wasn't sleepy. I went to the pail hung on the wall and was about to drink from the dripping ladle when the mother called: "Dina! Give him a glass."

"I don't need one," I said. "When I was a boy in the country I drank from the pail."

So I talked about our stables, the irrigated kitchen-gardens and the geese. "Thank goodness you've already been in the country," the mother said. "That way you're used to things; you know what's what."

We spoke of Pieretto who was used to another sort of life altogether and had lived only in cities. "However, he's not suffering any," I said, laughing. "He's never had it so good." And I told her about that crazy father of his who

70

had taken him about here and there, in monasteries, in villas, in garrets. "He's got the gift of gab and likes to make light of things, but it's all in fun," I said. "When you get to know him well, he grows on you."

The mother kneaded. "You and Pieretto will have to be satisfied with Oreste's company," she said. "We're just ignorant women."

Ignorance was the least of it. I didn't tell her, but I was glad that the women in the house were all elderly or only children. Imagine a young lady our own age, a sister of Oreste, with the gang of us around! Or a friend, another Carlotta! But the oldest girl was the eleven-year-old Dina, who at table had clapped her hand over her laughing mouth.

I asked if there was a tobacconist in the village, and the mother told Dina to accompany me. We went out together into the square and took the road I had taken in the morning. Now the wind had fallen; along one side of the square, in the shadow of the houses, women and old men took the air. We passed by the garden with the dahlias and I noticed that between one house and another you could see across the drop of the valley to further hills on a level with the village, like islands in the air. The people scanned us suspiciously; little Dina walked beside me, neat and clean, and chattered on about herself. I asked her where her father's vineyards were.

"The barn is at San Grato," she said, and pointed to the yellow back of our hill, which rose over the houses beyond the square. "That's one," she said. "That's where the white grapes are. Then there's Rossotto with the mill," and she indicated a declivity of meadows and thickets in the valley.

"Down there behind the station we have the festa. It's over for this year. There were fireworks. We saw them with mamma from the terrace. . . ."

I asked her who cultivated the land.

"Who?" She stopped amazed. "Why, the peasants," she said.

"I thought that perhaps you and your sister worked with your father."

Dina gave a snicker and looked at me dubiously. "Oh, really!" she said. "We haven't the time. We have to worry about whether they've done their work. Father directs them and sells the harvests."

"Would you like to work in the fields?"

"Oh no. You get all black. It's man's work."

When I came out of the tobacconist's, a basement shop smelling of sulphur and carob-beans, I found Dina waiting for me with a very serious expression.

"Lots of women go to the Riviera to sunbathe," I said. It's the style to be tanned. Have you ever seen the sea?"

All the way back, Dina talked about these things. She said she would go to the seaside when she got married, and not before. No one goes alone, and who would take her now? Oreste couldn't, for he was a young man.

"Your mother."

Dina said that her mother was too old-fashioned. She said that you had to get married before you could do anything like that.

"Shall we visit the church?" I asked then.

The church was in the square, large, and made of white stone, with saints and angels in niches. I held up the door-curtain and Dina squeezed by, crossed herself and knelt down. We looked about for a moment in the cool and coloured shade. At the far end the altar gleamed whitely, like a piece of nougat; and there were many flowers and a small lamp.

"Who brings the flowers for the Madonna?" I whispered.

"Little girls."

"Don't you get tanned from collecting flowers in the fields?" I asked softly.

When we came out, we bumped into an old lady in the doorway—Giustina. She moved away stiffly, then she recognized me and the child, and moved her lips in a quick smile. I took advantage of her surprise to go down the steps. But Giustina no longer had control of herself and she turned round and said: "There! That was the proper thing to do. God is always first. Have you seen the priest yet?"

I stammered that I had gone in out of simple curiosity, without any intentions.

"Whatever are you saying?" she said. "There is nothing to be ashamed of. You've done the proper thing. You've consoled me so much. . . ."

We left her on the steps, and as we crossed the square Dina told me that the old woman was in the rectory at all hours, and she would drop the housework—laundry, dishes, or cooking—so that she would not miss any of the functions. "If we all did that," Dina's mother used to say; "what would happen to the house?"

"It would go to heaven," Giustina would reply.

Other things happened that day, other meetings, and in the evening we ate and drank and then wandered about the village under the stars. I thought about it all the next day, lying naked in a dry basin under the ferocious sun, while

The Devil in the Hills

Oreste and Pieretto wallowed about like children. Under the broiling heat in the bed of the stream, I saw a sky colourless from so much light, and I felt the earth tremble and hum. I thought of Pieretto's remark that the red-hot countryside under the August sun makes one think of death. He wasn't wrong. The thrill we got out of lying there naked and knowing it, out of hiding ourselves from everyone's sight and browning ourselves like tree-trunks had a touch of the sinister about it: it was more bestial than human. On the high wall of the fissure, I could see the outcroppings of roots and filaments like black tentacles: the earth's internal secret life. Oreste and Pieretto, more used to the place than I, jumped about, waded in the pools and talked. And they made fun of my still pallid—shameful—parts.

No one could catch us unaware, for when you walk through millet, it gives off a noisy roaring. We were safe. Oreste, lying in the water, said: "Get tanned all over. We'll end up like bulls."

Down there it was strange to think about the world above, about people and life. The first evening we had wandered through the village to the retaining wall of the square, excited by the wine and the cool air, and we had said good evening to people, laughed and listened to singing. A group of young men shouted to Oreste; the parish priest walked in the shadows and watched us. The words and jokes we had exchanged under the stars with a woman and an old man, without seeing their faces clearly, and those we had exchanged among ourselves had given me a strange happiness, a festive and carefree sensation which the buffets of warm wind, the wheeling of the stars and distant lights increased to embrace the future, life. The

74

children in the square chased one another deafeningly. We made plans, learned the names of the hamlets scattered on the hillsides and hilltops, talked about the wines to drink, the pleasures awaiting us, the vintage.

"When September comes," Oreste said, "We'll go hunting."

Then I remembered Poli.

11

Wₑ began to talk about him at once, to the accompaniment of the crickets.

"The Greppo's down there," Oreste said, "below that cluster of stars. It rises just a bit above the edge of the down. You can make out the tops of the pines in the early morning. . . ."

"Let's go on over. Come on," Pieretto said.

But Oreste said that it wasn't worthwhile going at night and that Poli was surely still on the Riviera.

"If he hasn't died," Pieretto said.

"He was getting better. He's probably healed by now
. . . ."

"Some other girl may have shot him."

"Does it always have to happen to him?"

"What!" Pieretto cried into the wind. "Don't you know that what happens to you once, goes on happening to you? Or that if you act a certain way once, you always act that way. It's no fluke when you find yourself in a mess. And you go on finding yourself in the same mess over and over again. It's called destiny."

The day following, after we had come back from the cleft, we talked about Poli at table. Oreste said to the circle of faces: "You know whom I saw in Turin this year?"

After he had told, amidst an uproar of eager questions and exclamations, the story of the shooting and of Rosalba,

the green car. the night drives, his mother, during an
incredulous pause said:

"And he was such a beautiful baby! I remember him
when they used to drive by in the carriage with their para-
sols open. There was a wet-nurse in lace, with large safety
pins . . . she used to carry him. . . . It was the year I was
expecting Oreste."

"Are you sure it's Poli of the Greppo?" the father asked
quickly.

Oreste began again from that night on the hill.

"But this woman, who *is* she?" his mother asked, pallid.

The children listened with their mouths open.

"I feel sorry for his father," Oreste's father said. "A man
who owned nearly all Milan. You see the sort of thing that
can happen because of money."

"No, not what happens because of money," Pieretto said.
"Just the opposite. His father settled up everything. These
things happen in good families."

"Not here among us," Oreste said.

Old Giustina joined in. Until then she had been listening,
like a hawk, looking from one to the other of us.

"He's right," she said, looking sharply at Pieretto. "These
sins are committed everywhere. If parents would take care
of their children and discipline them instead of letting them
run free. . . ."

She continued for a bit. She became incensed again about
dancing and sea-bathing. Several words from her sister
accompanied by significant glances at the children, at Dina,
didn't stop her. But old Sabina—I don't know whether she
was a servant, a grandparent or an aunt—at the other end

of the table, blinking her eyes, interrupted to ask whom they were talking about.

They shouted something. Then she said angrily, in her strident voice, that the house at the Greppo was open, that the dressmaker's husband at the station had seen the trunks arrive, and that he didn't know about the young man, but there were certainly women up there.

That afternoon we went up to San Grato, on the back of the hill behind the village, where Oreste's father, who had been out on his property since the siesta hour, welcomed us. His peasants were spraying the rows of vines with Bordeaux mixture; bent under the canicular heat, they moved about in blouses and trousers hardened and splashed with blue, pumping the blue water from the brass sprays on their backs. The vine-leaves dripped, the pumps squeaked. We stopped above the great reservoir full of pure water, deep and opaque, like a blue eye, like a sky reversed. I remarked to Oreste's father that it was strange that they had to spray that poisonous rain on the grapes: the peasants' hats were all eaten away by it. "Once they grew grapes without all this," I said.

"They may have," he said, and then shouted something to a boy who was putting a bottle down in the grass. "They may have once. Now the vines are riddled with disease." He looked doubtfully at the sky. "Let's hope it doesn't rain," he cried. "It washes the mixture off the vines and then you have to do it all over again."

Oreste and Pieretto called me from above; they were under a tree, jumping to touch the bottom branches. "If you want any plums, you'd better get up there," he said. "That is if the birds left any."

I crossed the parched stubble and met them on the crest. It was like being in the sky. At our feet, diminished by distance, we could see the village square and a jungle of roofs, ladders, haystacks. You felt you wanted to jump from hill to hill, to embrace everything in a single glance. I looked east, along the level of the down, trying to locate the tops of the pines of the Greppo. The great light was entrapped down there, in the hollow between the hillsides, and the horizon wavered. I had to half-close my eyes, but I made out only haze.

Jumping from clod to clod, Oreste's father made his way up to us.

"It's magnificent country," Pieretto said with his mouth full. "You're crazy not to live here, Oreste."

"My idea was," the father said looking at his son, "that this young man should go to an agricultural college. Every day it becomes more difficult to make the land yield everything it should."

"In my village," I put in, "they say that peasants know more than agronomists."

"That's good horse sense," the father said. "Practice comes first of course. But nowadays everything is done with chemicals and fertilizers. And since he was going to college anyhow, he might just as well have studied how to get his property to yield everything it should as to study medicine, which is something that benefits others more than himself."

"Medicine's a sort of agriculture too," Oreste said. "A healthy body is like a farm that gives a high yield."

"But you'd better show yourself wide awake or I won't leave you the farm."

"Do the vines get many diseases?" Pieretto put in.

79

The Devil in the Hills

The father looked down at the farm spread below us and ran his eyes along the rows of vines whence rose innocent little clouds. "Oh, yes," he said. "The earth gets worn out. Perhaps it's true, as your friend says, that the countryside was healthier once, but now if you turn your back for a moment one day, you find everything diseased the next. . . ."

I didn't look at Pieretto, but I felt that he was smiling sarcastically.

"The earth is like a woman," the father continued. "You're young men now, but you'll know in good time. Women have something the matter with them every day: headaches, backaches, their moons. . . . Oh yes, it must be the effect of the month, the moon that waxes and wanes . . . ." He winked at us melancholically.

Pieretto again smiled sarcastically.

"But you," he attacked me suddenly, "what's all this you've been saying about the countryside changing? Men make the country. Plows, Bordeaux mixture, paraffin oil make it. . . ."

"Of course," Oreste said.

His father agreed.

". . . There's nothing mysterious about the country," Pieretto went on. "Even the mattock is a scientific instrument."

"I never said that the land had changed," I protested.

"Good God," the father put in, "you'll see how little a mattock counts when a field goes to bramble. You can't recognize it any more. It's like a desert."

It was my turn to smile sarcastically. I said nothing, but laughed.

He said: "The cleft is something else again."

80

"What?"

"It's different from these vineyards, for example. Here man reigns. Down there the toad."

"You find toads and snakes everywhere in the country," I said. "And crickets and moles. And the plants are the same everywhere. Day and night. The same roots that you find here grow in uncultivated land too."

The father listened to us thoughtfully. Turning round, he said suddenly: "If you want to see uncultivated land, go to the Greppo. Good God, all day I've been thinking about that boy and his father. Now I can understand certain things. When his grandfather was alive, they had to buy only two things to live on that farm—oil and salt. It's a shocking thing to have land and not live on it. . . ."

12

Every day we would go down to the cleft, talking and laughing as we walked along. It was beautiful to find the fields on eastern slopes still wet with morning dew; at times, the earth in the hot cavity would feel damp and nocturnal beneath my back and legs. We now knew every cranny in the thicket, every light, every noise and rustling of the morning. There were times when a large, white cloud would pass, opaque from the water it held; and then the upside-down images of the bank, of flowers, of the sky, would become more intense when the shadow moved away.

The sunbathing nearly became a vice, though by now we were brown all over. When for the first time we gave up the cleft to spend Sunday midday in front of the church among the festive crowd and attend mass from the doorway, among a confusion of kids, organ music and bells, I keenly missed not being naked and crushed between the sun and earth. I never told anyone the things I thought.

To Pieretto, who silently regarded the nape of Oreste's neck, I whispered: "Could you imagine these people being naked in the sun like us?"

He didn't bat an eyelash, and I returned to my thoughts. One day in the vineyard—we used to spend the afternoons at San Grato, and Pieretto was off by himself that day—I asked Oreste if there was any cranny, bank, or uncultivated spot in the country where no one had ever set foot, where, from the beginning of time, the rain, the sun and the seasons succeeded one another without the knowledge of man. Oreste said no, that there was not the remotest spot or centre of a wood which man's hand or eye had not disturbed. Hunters at least—and in other times bandits—have been everywhere.

But the peasants, the peasants, I said. Hunters didn't count. The hunter lives on his game. I wanted to know if the peasant as such had penetrated every spot, if everywhere the earth had been touched. Or, better still, violated.

Oreste said: "Who knows?" But he didn't understand. He shook his head and gave me his mother's sly glance.

We had been seated on the edge of the vineyard and raising your eyes you could see the vines move. Looking at a vineyard from below as it rises towards the sky, you seem to be out of the world. Under your feet you have chalky clouds, twisted vine-stocks, and above your eyes, a flight of green festoons and evenly spaced bamboo rods which touch the sky. You breathe and listen.

"That waggon-driver I saw at the station," I said suddenly; "he said that there have always been vineyards."

"Life used to be so easy in the old days," Oreste said. "Then you tied up the vines with sausage strings and milk flowed out at the foot."

"Nevertheless," I said, "even cities have always existed. They may have been dirty, made of straw, three huts, a cave. But 'man' means 'city.' You have to admit that Pieretto is right."

Oreste shrugged his shoulders. That was his way of discussing things, and it was as good as another.

"I wonder how bored he gets when mother closes the

door at midnight?" he said. "It was at night that Turin became his."

"Some night we'll have to go out," I said. "I'd like to see the hills under the moon. There was a sliver last night."

"You know, we went swimming by moonlight," Oreste said. "It's like drinking cold milk."

They had never told me. I felt a sudden sadness. I felt myself without a town, and jealous.

"The time is flying by," I said, "and yet these grapes never ripen. When do we go back to Turin?"

Oreste wouldn't hear of it. He asked me what else I could want: I ate, drank good wine and did nothing all day long. . . .

"But that's just the trouble. And your mother has more work to do. They all have to work for us."

"Are you bored?" Oreste asked. "Do you think you're giving too much trouble? . . . . Aunt Giustina likes you."

(It was I who had suggested that we attend mass; it was to show some regard for the family, nothing else).

"Aren't we going to the Mill today?"

Every day we would go down the hill into the hollow where the other barn was; we would walk about on the threshing-floor behind the peasants; Oreste's father would come out from the arches and offer us wine. But the beauty of Rossotto was in the haying, the long fields of clover and the geese. Towards evening we would play a round at bowls with the hired hands, Pale and Quinto; and Oreste would go to the station on private affairs.

"I say something stinks," Pieretto said. "When he was in Genoa he was sending letters every day."

When we said anything about it to Oreste, he would

laugh and shake his head. And he gave us the same smile when, walking along the railway, we passed before a house with pots of geraniums on the window-sills and he shouted a greeting and a fresh, happy, feminine voice answered him. He told us to go on and he turned round the corner.

"Well, then," Pieretto said, when Oreste arrived on the threshing-floor, "it must be the stationmaster's daughter?"

Oreste laughed again but didn't say a word. But there was something like a propitious sky over the hollow in which the Mill stood. Even at the level crossing where the carts stopped and the animals dropped dung, one breathed a different sort of gentleness: the flower-boxes and flower-beds of the station made you think of city outskirts, the girls walking of a May evening along the avenues when the smell of hay invests the city. For all their being shirtless and shoeless, the hired hands at Rossotto also felt the effect of the trains and talked about beer and bike races.

In the evening, after haying, we drank wine and not beer. Oreste's father had said to us, "Come up before dinner." And with his jacket over his shoulder he had started up the path. There was a certain festive activity at the station and Oreste begged our pardon for an absence longer than usual. The cellars of Rossotto yielded one bottle and then another. As you drank, the wine left your mouth drier and drier. We three drank, seated under the arches which gave on the fields. Did all that sweetness pass from the wine into the air, or vice versa? For it was like drinking the perfume of hay.

"It's strawberry wine," Oreste said. "From my cousins at Mombello."

"We're fools," Pieretto said. "Day and night we search

85

for the secret of the country, and we have it right here inside."

Then we wondered why we had never got drunk since we had come to the country though we liked to spend evenings in wineshops in Turin.

"We'll have to go out some night," I said. "We can't get drunk in your house."

"Come off it," Oreste said. "Consider it your own home."

The conversation turned to horses. At Rossotto there was a gig that would seat three, and Oreste said that all we had to do was hitch it up and we'd go off right away.

"Let's go and visit my cousins at Mombello," he said. "I'd like to see them. They've got heads on their shoulders, all right. We can leave in the morning and be back in the evening."

"We'll miss our sun-bath," I muttered. "I missed out this morning."

Pieretto grunted. "Who gives a damn? I'm sick of seeing you naked."

"That's your loss," I said.

"But you're no gift to anyone's eyes," he shouted. "I can't stand seeing you any more except when I'm drunk."

Oreste filled our glasses.

"Some things just can't be done," I said suddenly. "You can't go naked in the woods and fill yourself with wine."

"Why not?" Oreste said.

"Nor make love in the woods. In real woods. Love and drinking are civilised things. When I went boating——"

Pieretto interrupted. "You never understand anything."

"When you went boating? . . . ." Oreste said.

"I had a girl with me and she was willing. She would have done it. Well, *I* couldn't. It seemed to me that I would offend someone or something."

"That's because you don't know what a woman is," Pieretto said.

"But you don't mind being naked in the cleft?" Oreste asked.

I confessed that I didn't, but that my breath caught in my throat. "I feel as though I'm committing a sin," I admitted. "Perhaps that's why it's pleasant."

Oreste nodded, smiling. I realized that we were drunk. "The proof is," I continued, "that we do these things secretly."

Pieretto said that there are lots of things you do secretly which are not sinful. It is a question of custom and good manners. Sin is only when you do not understand what you are doing.

"Take Oreste," he said. "Every day he secretly goes to visit his girl. She's not far from here. They do nothing obscene. They talk in the garden, perhaps they hold hands. She asks him when he will have his degree and she will have him all to herself. He replies that it is a matter of another year, then there is the military service, then he has to find his probationer's post: three years? All right? And he waddles over to her importantly and kisses her tresses . . . ."

Oreste, scarlet, shook his head and took hold of the bottle.

". . . And you call this sin?" Pieretto said, moving away. "This little scene, this society game—sin? . . . But he might at least take us into his confidence and tell us all about it. He's not a real friend. Tell us something about her, Oreste. Her name at least."

Blushing, Oreste smiled. "Some other time," he said. "Let's drink this evening."

13

But I had already learned everything from Dina one day when I had found her seated on a stool on the terrace, sewing.

"Well, soon you'll be getting married," I said.

"It's your turn first," she retorted. "You're a young man."

"But young men have plenty of time," I said. "Look at Oreste; he's not even thinking of marriage."

A little game of gibes and replies followed, and Dina enjoyed my surprise. In a low, sly voice she let the cat out of the bag. She told me that Oreste was courting Cinta; Cinta's parents knew it, but no one here at home knew. Cinta was the daughter of the road maintenance man and worked at the dressmaker's; she was very good at it and made her own dresses and rode about on a bicycle. Dina even knew that Oreste had to pretend in front of the townspeople that he was only flirting, as Cinta's father tilled his vineyards by himself.

"Is she pretty?" I asked her. "Do you like her?"

Dina shrugged her shoulders. "Oh, I like her all right. But Oreste's the one who has to marry her."

And Dina had also realized that we were drunk the evening after haying.

"Last night we were talking to Oreste about Cinta," I whispered to her on the steps where we had sat down under the slice of moon.

She stared at me with her large eyes. "You had some wine? How many bottles?"

"How do you know?"

"All during dinner you covered your glass with your hand."

I wondered what sort of woman little Dina would be. I looked at the old women, Giustina, the others, Oreste's mother; I compared them with the village girls whom you saw working in the fields, strong legs, dark, broad faces, of good blood. It was the wind, the hill and their thick blood that made them so hard and sturdy. At times when I was drinking or eating—soup, meat, peppers, bread—I wondered what effect that rough, substantial food—earthy juices which were the same that passed in the wind—would have had on my blood.

And yet Dina was blonde, tiny, a wasp. Cinta too, I thought, would be fragile and slim, a grapevine. "Perhaps she eats only bread and peaches."

A storm, fortunately without hail, came and beat the countryside and eroded the paths and roads. It was the morning that we were to have gone off in the gig. We spent it in the house, moving from one window to another, among the women and children who ran about and complained at the flashes of lightning. Oreste's father had put on his boots and gone out immediately. The crackling vine faggots in the fireplace threw fantastic reflections on the scalloped shelf-linings of coloured paper, the battery of copper pans, the coloured lithographs of the Madonna and the olive branch hung on the wall. An odour of garlic and basil rose from the pieces of rabbit on the bloody trencher. The windows rattled. Someone upstairs shouted to us to close the windows.

"And Giustina's out in this!" someone shouted up the stairs.

"Don't worry," the voice of Oreste's mother replied. "She always has a place where she can get in out of the rain."

A moment of strange solitude—almost of peace and silence—came in the flood. I stood at the bottom of the stairs and looked up to see drops of water rushing down the slope of the darkened skylight. You could hear the mass of water, almost solid, fall and rumble. I imagined the smoking and flooded fields, the boiling cleft, the uncovered roots, and the most private spots of the earth now penetrated and violated.

It ended as it had begun, suddenly. When we went out onto the terrace with Dina and the other women—you heard people calling to one another all over the village—the leaf-scattered paving already had dry spots. A frothy wind blew up from the valley, and the clouds rushed along. The sea of nearly black hills speckled with whitish clay seemed nearer than usual. But I was not surprised by the clouds or the horizon. A heavy odour, a mixture of wetness, bracken and crushed flowers—a sharp, almost salty, odour of lightning and rootstocks—assailed me. Pieretto said: "How delightful!" Even Oreste inhaled and laughed.

That morning we didn't go to the cleft; Oreste's father called us to San Grato to inspect the damage. Up there the fruit had been slaughtered and some roof tiles broken. Together with the children, we gathered up large baskets of bespattered apples and peaches from the mud. We re-tied some beaten down vines. It was beautiful to see certain tiny flowers hanging to half-dissolved clods raise themselves delicately, miraculously, in the sun. The thick blood of the earth was capable of this too. Everyone said that the woods would soon be filled with mushrooms.

We didn't go collecting mushrooms. Instead we went to visit Oreste's cousins the next day. The little horse, following the left-hand fork at the station, took us along a faint rise covered with expanses of millet, some small woods, and more millet. The morning sun had already worked miracles. If it hadn't been for the scabrous crust on the road and the odour of the wind, no one would have said that it had rained the day before. We ran between fields, up slight rises, now under the light shadow of acacias, now boxed in by cane-brakes.

The farm was at the end of the down, amidst low hills, hidden by giant reeds and oaks. As we approached, I turned round now and then because Oreste, shortly before, had pointed off towards the skyline and said: "There's the Greppo." An enormous woody slope, dark with damp, rose just above the vines against the sky. It seemed uninhabited, without a roof or a tilled field.

"Can that be the estate?" I muttered.

"The villa is at the top, hidden behind the trees. You can see the villages in the plain from up there."

We went down into a depression and the Greppo was hidden, and we arrived at the barn while I was still trying to make it out among the trees.

At first I didn't understand why Oreste was so enthusiastic about his cousins. They were grown men—one even had some grey hair—with large, hairy hands. Dressed in chequered shirts and fustian, they came out into the barnyard and without showing any surprise took the horse by the bridle.

"It's Oreste," they said.

"Davide! Cinto!" Oreste shouted, jumping to the ground.

Three hunting dogs ran up, growling a bit and leaping round Oreste. It was a large barnyard of brown, almost red, earth, like the vineyards along which we had driven. The house was of stone, stained blue by the Bordeaux mixtur sprayed on the espaliered vines. A ground floor window looked out, empty, black.

First the horse was led into the shade under the oaks and left there to paw and quiet down.

"All doctors?" Davide asked, raising his eyes.

Oreste explained who we were.

"Let's go where it's cool," Cinto said, starting off.

That day we were drinking again, and August has long days. Now and then one of the cousins got up and disappeared into a sort of grotto and came out with a dark glass. Then we too descended into the cellar, and here Davide filled our frosted glasses at the cask, making a hole in the mastic and then plugging it with his finger. But this was in the afternoon. In the meantime, we had wandered about the house and the vineyards, eaten a lunch of polenta, salami and melons, caught sight of women and children in the dark. The room was low, rustic as a stable: we went out and saw clouds of starlings rise from the fields dotted with oaks.

Next to the stable there was a well and Davide drew up a bucket of water and threw some bunches of white grapes into it and told us to eat them. Pieretto, seated on a stump, laughed like a child and talked with his mouth full. Cinto, the younger of the two, walked about the well, listened to the conversation and regarded the horse complacently.

We talked about everything that day; that is, about harvests, hunting, the storm, the year's crops.

"You'll be shut in here during winter," I had said. "You're in low land."

"If we have to, we'll go to higher land," Davide said.

Oreste said: "Don't you know that winter's their best season? Do you have any idea how beautiful it is to go hunting in the snow?"

"It's beautiful all year round," Davide added. "When the day goes well."

It seemed as though the bitches understood. They had got up and looked at us restlessly.

"But there aren't any game wardens here," Pieretto said. "I wonder how many hares you shoot in August?"

"Tell that to Cinto," Davide broke into laughter. "Tell that to Cinto; he's always shooting pheasants."

Then Oreste raised his head as though catching a scent. "Are there still pheasants on the Coste?" He tried to catch the eyes of Davide and Cinto. "Did you know that Poli of the Greppo was shot at?—like a pheasant?"

The pair listened silently. While Oreste excitedly told the story, Davide poured him a glass. I became aware as I listened that the story, now old, had an unreal, discordant air. What could it have in common with that wine, that earth, those two?

When Oreste had finished, he looked first at the brothers and then at us.

"You forgot to say that he takes coke," Pieretto commented.

"Oh yes," Oreste said. "His brains are really a bit addled."

"He knows what he's doing," Davide said. "It's a good job he's on his feet now."

"We're not sure whether he's returned to the Greppo," Oreste said.

"He's there, all right," Cinto said quietly. "They do their shopping at Due Ponti."

"What does the caretaker say?" Oreste asked, surprised.

Cinto smiled reticently.

Davide replied for him: "There was an argument over the cane-brake. There was so much fuss that we had to put him off our land. That chap keeps an eye on the brake. But you know how it is. . . . It's something you don't talk about."

14

We left under a bit of moon in the cool, late afternoon air. We were sorry to leave that island, that immense red countryside with its thin, black vines under the oaks.

"Let's go before it get's dark," Oreste said.

The horse shot off like a hunting dog. As he ran under an apple tree, Pieretto raised his hand and grabbed an apple.

"Oh-ho!" we shouted, smacking our tongues.

"Have you ever drunk so much wine?" Pieretto said. "And carried it so well?"

"When you drink in the open air," Oreste said, "you can't get drunk."

Then winking at one another, they asked me: "What do you say now? You claim you don't like to drink or make love in the country. . . . What do you say now?"

I brushed the question aside as you brush away a fly. "I like those two," I said into the wind that rushed by.

Then we talked about Davide and Cinto, the wines, the grapes in the bucket, about how fine genuine life is.

"The great thing is the way they keep their women," Pieretto said. "We were outside drinking and telling stories and they and the brats were in the kitchen, but they weren't breaking their hearts."

The low sun raked across the vineyards and dug out a redness, a rich shadow, from each clod and trunk.

96

"Anyhow, they work," I said. "They've made this earth what it is."

"Don't be an ass, Oreste," Pieretto said. "The devil with Turin. The devil with the anatomy hall. You ought to marry that girl and cultivate your lands in peace. . . ."

With his eyes fixed on the neck of the horse, following the curve of the road with his chin, Oreste said calmly: "Who says I don't want to? . . . Give me time."

"What a queer sort you are!" I observed. "Your fathers want you to be monks and agronomists. You won't hear of it; you worry them no end. And Pieretto will end up a monkish atheist and Oreste a country doctor."

Pieretto smiled complacently. "Everyone ought to help his father," he said. "He's got to be taught that life is hard. If afterwards, as is only right, you do what he wants, you have to convince him that he was wrong to want it and that you did it only for his sake.

"Are you really going to marry that girl?" I asked Oreste.

"Don't ask him now. Don't ask him now," Pieretto said. "He's got the excuse that he's drunk."

In the early evening the moon was beautiful, a colour between white and yellow, and I began to think of its nocturnal rays over the immense countryside, on the earth, on the hedges. I remembered the slope of the Greppo too late and I saw it disappear over our shoulders in the pure air. "Was that the Coste?" I was about to ask, but at that moment Oreste spoke.

"Her name's Giacinta," he said without looking at us. Then shouting and snapping the whip: "Good God, I'm going mad this year!"

The night before, he and Pieretto couldn't sleep and they had begun to talk about life at the seaside. Oreste had said that the low hills through which we were now driving had seemed to him from the time that he was a child a marine horizon—a mysterious sea of islands and distances into which he had in his imagination dived from the height of the terrace. "God, how I wanted to be on the go, take a train, see things and do things. Now I feel good here. I don't even know if I like the sea."

"But you took to it like a fish," Pieretto said.

We arrived at Rossotto singing and after the last bit on foot, we decided to drink some more. Women understand these things and they put a table and a bottle of wine on the terrace for us. Oreste's mother said: "Now you'd better take your moon cure. The moon's heard plenty by now."

There was no wind, the village slept, dogs barked somewhere. It was Oreste's night, he told us all about Giacinta. When the moon went down and the cock crew, Pieretto said: "God. You've put some heart into me too."

The next day was Sunday. How the weeks went by! Again we walked about the square among the strange men and the veiled girls who made you think of the great sun and the cleft. That was how we attended mass—looking at the sky. I wondered if the two taciturn cousins at Mombello were the sort to take a holiday, if they were in the habit of interrupting their lives on the threshing-floor and in the fields and wine cellar to mingle among other people. Hunting, patient waiting and evening solitude were their holidays. When the church emptied, I looked at the faces one by one to see if I could find someone else with an

expression or bearing so reticent, quiet and savage as theirs.
Our women came out. Giustina looked at us intently, jerk-
ing the children along, and began an argument.

She wanted to know why we came at all since we missed
mass afterwards by standing outside the holy ground.

"What's the holy ground?" Oreste asked.

Pieretto was the most outrageous. He explained that the
whole world is God's temple and that even Saint Francis
knelt in the forest.

"Saint Francis was a saint," Giustina growled. "He
believed in God."

Pieretto said that people who go into churches don't
believe in God. "Don't tell me that the rector believes in
God," he declared. "Not with that face."

Round about us they were discussing coming holidays
and fairs, for the end of August is an empty time in which
the country, between grain harvest and vintage, takes a
breath and the peasants move about, make contracts, enjoy
life and let things slide. There were festas everywhere, and
they were all talking about going to them.

"The service," Giustina said. "The service. If you don't
respect the ministers of the service, you are neither Christian
nor Italian."

"Religion," Oreste's father said, "isn't just going to
church. Religion is a difficult thing. It's raising children,
maintaining a family, living peacefully with everyone. . . ."

And Giustina said to Pieretto: "Well, let's hear what you
have to say," she cried. "What is religion?"

"Religion," Pieretto said, stopping, "is understanding
how things go. Holy water is no use. You have to speak

99

with people, understand them, know what each of them wants. They all want something out of life, they want to do something—exactly what, they're never sure of. Well, it is in this intent that they all find God. It is enough to understand, and to help others to understand. . . ."

"And when you're dead," Oreste remarked, "what have you understood?"

"You damned grave-digger!" Pieretto said. "When you're dead you have no more intentions."

They continued at table and after. Pieretto said that he admitted the saints; or, rather, that there wasn't anything but saints, for everyone in his intention resembles a saint, and if he were only allowed to do what he liked, he would bear fruit. But instead, priests cling to some famous saint and say: "Do as he did; he is enough to save us," and they take no account of the fact that there are no two drops of water alike in the whole world and that each day is different.

Now Giustina kept quiet, throwing glances at us. At four o'clock we were seated on the terrace having coffee, and faint voices, rustlings and gusts of wind rose out of the burning sea of the countryside. From the shade where we were sitting you could see the slopes of the valleys, great flanks like those of recumbent cows. Each hill was a world in itself, made up of successive places, slope and plain, spotted with vineyards, fields, coppices. There were houses, clumps of thicket, horizons. Even after you looked at it a great deal you always discovered something new—an unusual tree, the turn in a path, a threshing-space, a colour not noticed before. From the west, the sun threw every small thing into relief, and even the strange sea corridor, the vague cloud over the Greppo was closer to the summit than usual. We would have to go next day in the gig, and meanwhile anything we talked about served to pass the evening.

15

The hill of the Greppo was also a world. To get there we went along the Coste, along declivities and solitary slopes, beyond the region of the oaks. When we arrived under the side of the Greppo, we saw the black, luminous trees on the crest etched against the sun. From a bend half-way up the road Oreste showed us how far Poli's lands extended in the countryside through which we had driven. We had got out of the gig, which followed at our own pace, and walked along a road much wider than the previous one. This wide road—still with some patches of asphalt here and there—cut across the wild hillsides thick with briars and trees. But the astonishing thing was the tangle, the abandonment: we passed some deserted vineyards overgrown with grass and came to a thick wood where fruit trees—fig and cherry overgrown with creepers—mingled with willows and acacias, plane-trees and elders. At the beginning of the rise there was a wood of hornbeams and gloomy, almost cold, poplars; then little by little as we came out into the sun, the vegetation grew thinner and unusual trees such as oleanders, magnolias, cypresses and others I had never seen before were added to the familiar ones in a disorder which gave an air of exotic solitude to the glades.

"Is this what your father meant?" I asked Oreste.

He told me that we had already passed the real waste, the woodland and plowland plain where everybody pastured and cut firewood as they pleased. "They wanted to make a hunting reserve here. You can see the road they built. When Poli's grandfather ran things, he used to have large parties of guests here. But in those days the plain was cultivated and the old man went around with a gun and whip day and night. My dad knew him. He was from down there."

I was at once struck by the odour in the air, a mixture of scorched vegetable fermentation, earth and sun, and the burning breath of the asphalt. It was an odour which had a touch of motor cars, speed, coastal roads and gardens on the sea. A hedge of prickly-pear hung from an embankment above the road.

We came out at the top among bushes, and here the thicket became a real park, a pinewood which circled the villa. Now we had gravel under our feet, and the sky showed through the tree tops.

"It's like an island," Pieretto said.

"A natural skyscraper," I added.

"The way it is now," Oreste said, "it's no use to anyone. It would be a good place for a clinic, a modern clinic, with all the latest apparatus. Two steps from home—what do you say?"

"There's already an odour of death," Pieretto said.

The smell of rot came from a pool level with the ground, about ten yards square, with an accumulation in the centre and green, stagnant water, scattered with small white flowers.

"You have a swimming pool too," I said to Oreste. "You can throw your dead in there and pull them out alive."

We could glimpse the house among the pine trunks.

"Let's stop here," Oreste said. "I'll go and explore."

We remained alone with the horse, and I silently watched

the strange sky above the trees. I hoped that Poli wasn't there, that no one was there and that after taking a walk through the park we might go home. The odour of the pool had reminded me of the cleft and my heart grew nostalgic for country I knew. Had it been possible, I should have liked to have taken another look at the woods when we went down, for it was beautiful in its wild abandonment.

"Who are you looking for?" asked a clear voice.

She had approached among the trees, quietly, wearing a blouse and white shorts, a blonde girl with hard eyes.

We looked at one another. The tone of her voice told us that she was married. At that moment the horse and the gig seemed to me ridiculous.

"We're looking for Poli," Pieretto said with a smile. "We're——"

"Poli?" The woman raised her eyes, almost offended. So that I shouldn't stare at her legs, I looked to one side, and in every sense felt shabby.

"We're friends of Poli," Pieretto said. "We met him in Turin. We'd like to know how he is."

The woman didn't like that either, and her frown changed to a bored smile, and she looked at us impatiently.

At that moment Oreste burst out of the avenue, exclaiming agitatedly: "Poli's here and so is his wife. Who'd have thought he had a wife! . . . ."

Seeing the girl, he stopped.

"Did you find him?" Pieretto said, unruffled.

Colouring, Oreste stammered that the gardener had gone to search for him. He looked from us to the woman. He hesitated.

"We're trying to keep up a conversation," Pieretto said.

Suddenly the blonde became mollified. She eyed us skeptically and held out her hand. She was anything but grave.

"My husband's friends are my friends too," she said, laughing. "Here comes Poli."

I have thought many times since about that meeting. Oreste's reddening, and the days which followed up there. The girl Giacinta came immediately into my mind—I don't know why—but Giacinta was dark. Also the fact that Poli had a wife disturbed me at the moment. All our past with him became prohibited ground, became an obstacle. What could we talk about any more? We couldn't even ask him how his father was.

But Poli welcomed us with that faintly absurd exaggerated warmth which was characteristic of him. He didn't seem much changed; he was plump, with a soft, infantile expression. He wore a brief shirt outside his trousers and a thin chain round his neck. He told us immediately that we must stay at the villa, remain with him day and night; our long talks would do him good.

"But aren't you on your honeymoon?" Pieretto asked.

They looked at one another and then at us. Poli smiled, amused.

"Honey gives him hives," the woman said with faint regret. "All water under the bridge. We're here to be bored. I keep him company and act as his nurse a little."

"The wound must be healed by now," Oreste said.

Pieretto smiled.

Then Oreste understood, bit his lip and stammered:

"Your father's not an easy man to upset. But you've managed to give him grey hair. . . ."

The woman said: "You must be thirsty. Show them the way, Poli. I'll be right along."

So in the high, glass-enclosed room full of curtains and easy chairs, Poli continued to make much of us and to sigh happily, and when Pieretto asked whether his wife knew about everything, he said yes, quite simply. "There was a time when Gabriella and I told each other everything. She's been a great comfort to me, poor girl. We've done plenty of crazy things together, as all the world knows. Then life separated us. But now we've agreed to spend the summer together like the children we used to be. We have remembrances in common. . . ."

Pieretto stood listening with evident courtesy.

Oreste couldn't contain himself and burst out: "But what the devil were you doing in Turin if you were married?"

Poli looked at him with displeasure, almost with fear. He said merely: "You don't always do what others would like you to do."

Gabriella joined us and opened the liquor cabinet. It was lined with glass and lit up when opened. We talked about the Greppo. I said that it was very beautiful up there and that I could understand spending one's life wandering about in the forest.

"Yes, it might be pleasant," she said.

"What do you do here from morning to night?" Pieretto asked.

Slumped in her easy chair, Gabriella stretched out her bare legs. "We sunbathe, sleep, do exercises. . . . We don't see anyone."

I couldn't get used to her unpredictable, tanned and sly face. She was very young, she must have been younger than

Poli, but her voice at times had harsh inflexions which surprised me. From drinking? I thought; or from other things?

"We have a cold lunch," she told us, laughing. "Jam, biscuits. We have our main meal in the evening."

We protested that they were waiting for us at home. That the horse was waiting. We had to be back before dark.

Poli's face became pensive, he argued against our going. He told Pieretto that it was like a holiday to have us with him and that he had many things to tell us. He told his wife to give orders to prepare rooms for us.

We argued good-humouredly, but didn't yield. His insistence annoyed me, and, looking at Oreste, I thought of the road back, of the window awaiting him at the station, of the twilight.

Poli said: "What does it matter whose house you eat and sleep in? Why do you want to treat me like this?"

Gabriella raised her glass urbanely, looked at him with surprise and then said to us: "Do you find chickens and public dances so interesting?"

Even Poli laughed. We came to the understanding that we would return the next day for a longer visit.

16

It took us two days to convince Oreste's family to let us go back. "Aren't you comfortable here?" his father asked. The women, with disapproving faces, held a council at the table. Only the news that Poli was married pacified his mother; and then the conversation shifted to the new aspect which Poli's adventures had assumed, and they wanted to know if the wife was not, as was her duty, undone by distress, yet at the same time firm and resolved not to give in.

"She doesn't give a damn. She sunbathes," Oreste said.

"That's what happens when you separate from your husband."

"But when two people separate," his father said, "it means that there's something behind it all."

Oreste, annoyed, concluded that it was entirely the fault of money. "If you don't have too much money, then you study or work and you don't have the time for a lot of nonsense. . . . Well, are we going or aren't we?"

We left in the gig, but without having settled whether Oreste would stay over with us or not. During the good-byes that first afternoon, Gabriella had said that it was a shame not to be able to come and get us in the car, and Poli very quietly added that his father had taken it from him so that he wouldn't run any risks and would really rest. Once again we crossed the countryside, passed by the growths of oak, the broken hedges. I saw the hornbeams and the forest on the slope again. Everything was shining and dripping in the morning sun. The great brush-covered hill stood solitary amidst the humming of bees. My eyes searched out the abandoned glades. Pieretto said that it wasn't right that a whole hill should belong to one man, as in the times when a village bore the name of a single family. Birds flew about.

"Are they a part of the earth too?" I murmured.

On the level ground where the pines grew, we found something new. Deck-chairs and bottles and pillows lay abandoned on the turf. The gardener busied himself with the horse, taking it into the coach-house; Pinotta, a red-headed, sulky girl, who had already served us at table before, remained at the door of the offices and watched us without coming out into the sun.

"They're sleeping," she replied to our question, pointing her chin up towards the house. From the offices came the sound of water running on zinc.

"What a lot of bottles" Pieretto said sympathetically. "They must have drunk like pigs. . . . Was there a party last night?"

"A whole crowd came from Milan," the girl muttered, pushing back her hair with her arm. "They danced until daylight and had a pillow fight. What a mess! . . . . Are you staying?"

"Where are they now?" Oreste asked.

"They came and left in a car. . . . What people! One of the women fell out of the window."

The morning was cool in the pinewood. We smoked while we waited. No one in the house stirred. I went to lean against a tree and looked down on the plain. We drank

109

the dregs which still remained in a bottle of liqueur and asked Pinotta to open the verandah for us.

It was there that Poli and Gabriella found us. They announced themselves with a lot of noise, Pinotta ran up the stairs, we heard voices, bells, a slamming of doors. Finally Poli descended, in pyjamas, stammering, and with his hair mussed. He complained that we had made him wait three days, he shook hands; and so we stood talking about whether the blame for excesses should be placed on the seducer or on the one who allows himself to be seduced.

"Good friends," Poli. "They gave me a taste of what life's like in Milan. . . . I only hope they don't come back again. We should be by ourselves."

Gabriella entered, cool, wearing a blue dress. "Well, there! Come on. I daresay you'd like to bathe first," she said to us. "Let them alone, Poli. You can talk afterwards."

I had already forgotten her honey-blonde hair, her bare, sandalled feet, and her constant air of just having stepped onto a beach.

Leading us upstairs to our rooms, she said: "Let's hope none of those crazy people has slept over."

Then Oreste declared firmly that he would sleep at home: he would leave us at the Greppo and would come back on bicycle.

"Why?" Gabriella made a face. "Mamma doesn't want to lose you?" Then laughing, she added: "I'll leave you to do what you like. You know the way."

When I went down into the living room, I found them with Oreste. Pieretto had remained behind to wallow in the bath. He had shouted something to me through the door.

When I re-entered the glass-enclosed room, I had not yet

resigned myself to the adventure. Pinotta had by then finished setting the flower-vases straight, collected the plates and glasses and put away the ashtrays, and the room was a delightful place with pale curtains and graceful furniture. The other rooms held more rustic furnishings—seat lockers, chairs, huge oak tables and even a canopied bed—accumulated since the days of the hunting grandfather, but here in the living room you felt the hand of Gabriella and Poli. Or of Rosalba? I wondered. I couldn't get Rosalba, the spots of blood and the thoughtless malignity of those days out of my mind. The difficulty which I felt in walking on rugs, bearing myself civilly, seeing the unfortunate Pinotta called and ordered harshly or familiarly was increased by the memory of Rosalba, by the knowledge of what things could happen in the midst of all this cleanliness and civilised living.

That morning we talked about woods. Oreste happened to say that I liked the country so much that I had given up the sea to come here, and Gabriella immediately started to talk about the sea, about a friend's place, a beach with a small harbour, where the trunks of the olives descended the hill to the water. It was a private sea, a fenced-in beach, prohibited, and there was a swimming pool in the middle of the wood for use on windy days, and the swimmers along the coast could not bathe there, no one could who was not one of them. Poli berated the taste of the owners who, according to him, sent the servants about dressed as fishermen, with sashes about their waists and stocking caps on their heads.

"Don't be an ass. That was just that one time when they had that party," Gabriella said with a sharpness I found

111

displeasing. I caught a brief expression of malice on her face, as when we met her the first day.

Oreste said: "There were trees that went right down to the water?"

"There still are. Those things don't change." She had become calm again, but while she talked, she kept an eye on Poli's movements. He smoked and smiled abstractedly.

"Gabriella danced to Chopin among those trees," he said, looking fatuously at the smoke rising from his cigarette. "Classical dances under the moon, barefooted, with a veil. You remember, Gabri?"

"It's a shame your friends weren't here yesterday," she said to him.

She called Pinotta and told her to open the windows. "It still stinks from last night," she cried. "Erotics and drunks leave a place like animals. She was odious, that painter friend of yours, smoking her cigars."

"I should have thought' you would have held the orgy under the pines," I said.

"They were like monkeys," she flashed. "They disappeared all over the place. There might even be a couple in the woods now."

Poli smiled to himself. "Isn't Pieretto coming down?" he asked.

When Pieretto came into the room, Gabriella had already told Oreste and me that there was absolute freedom at the Greppo, you came and went as you liked, and if you wanted to be alone you could. "You come down, I go up," she said to Pieretto. "Be good, boys." She had disappeared the first day at the same hour; Poli had told us then that she sunbathed and we had talked about it in the gig and Pieretto

112

had said: "She has the stigmata too. . . . Shall we invite her to come along to the cleft?"

I should have liked to have gone off by myself at the time, to wander about the hill as I pleased until lunch time. Instead I took Oreste by the arm and we walked under the pines; Poli and Pieretto, who followed us, had begun to talk.

17

Towards dusk Oreste left in the gig, annoyed, and it was night on the Greppo. I managed to be alone under the pines, awaiting the dinner hour. Pieretto and Poli argued beside the pool. Poli, who had gone about all day with a tired and swollen face, spoke submissively—I was reminded of that night on the hill, the night Oreste had launched his hunting cries. I heard Pieretto's sallies from the other side of the hedge, his peremptory witicisms. Poli complained and talked about himself, his body. "When I understood that I had to get well, that I had to remake myself all over like a child. . . . There are certain things you never really know well. The idea of dying didn't frighten me. The difficult thing is to live. . . . I'm grateful to that poor girl for having taught me that much. . . ."

He spoke slowly, fervently, in his low, clear voice.

". . . At bottom in all of us there is a great peace, a joy. . . . And the rest of us is born from that. I understood that evil and death . . . do not come out of us—we do not create these things. . . . I forgive Rosalba, she wanted to help me. . . . Now everything has become easier, even Gabriella. . . ."

Pieretto had interrupted him with a growl. He said. "Nonsense!" It must have been right to Poli's face. The two voices clashed together for an instant and Pieretto's won.

"You've got some brass," he said. "You think I'll swallow that? Rosalba had no intention of helping you, and you

have no right to pity her. You were both a pair of pigs
. . . . Leave off all that gab about innocence."

Poli spoke in a low voice. ". . . It was all destined. We
are not condemned to death by ourselves. . . ."

The voices retreated under the moon. I sniffed the odour
of the pines in the still warm air. It was nearly a seaside
odour, pungent. During the day we had wandered about in
the thickets, going half way down the hillside. Gabriella
had taken us under a tufa overhang to a small grotto ringed
with maidenhair, where a bit of water gathered. We found
some peaches in a tree in a hollow, honey-ripe. For some
secret reason, Oreste was excessively gay. He let out some
of his wild cries to scare Gabriella. Towards evening I
became aware that barnyard sounds could not be heard
from the Greppo—the singing of birds, cock crows, bark-
ing. Up there you dominated the plain as from a cloud.

When it was dark, we went in to dine at the glistening
table Pinotta had prepared in the dining room. Pinotta was
afraid of Gabriella's glances and hustled about. "Table is
sacred," Gabriella had said. "As long as you're able you
should make a feast of each mouthful." She insisted that
flowers should be scattered here and there, thrown down
felicitously upon the tablecloth. She came down in sandals
and a green dress and said amiably: "Do sit down." I tried
not to look at Pieretto's cuffs.

We talked about Oreste and his secretive mood, about
when he and Poli used to flush partridge in the under-
growth. We talked about city and country living. We talked
about Poli as a boy and of the need for solitude which
sooner or later seizes everybody. Gabriella chattered about
trips, the annoyances of the fashionable world, strange en-

115

counters in mountain hotels. She had been born in Venice. We confessed to being merely two students.

And all the time Pinotta served us, with the shuffling step of one walking barefoot. I knew that somewhere in the kitchen there was another one like her, a cook, the real mistress of the house. I looked at the flowers on the white tablecloth, I swallowed noiselessly, watched Gabriella out of the corner of my eye. I could still hardly believe that I was there, that such a house should rise like an island in that peasant land. I recalled the scallops of coloured paper on the mantel of Oreste's fireplace, the yellow millet on the threshing floor, the vineyards, the faces in the doorways. Gabriella ate resignedly, Poli bent over his plate, and we all listened to Pieretto who went on and on about how he liked to walk at night.

I watched Gabriella out of the corner of my eye and wondered if, after all, Oreste hadn't been cleverer than we had. With a fine show of manners, Oreste had returned home to sleep on it, to be alone and to think about it from a distance. He knew Poli better than we did, he knew other things besides, and it was clear that he didn't really care to stay at the Greppo. He hadn't gone back just in order to run to Giacinta. Two days before, when we had been wondering whether Gabriella merited coming with us to the cleft, we had talked about them. But what are those two doing here in the country? we had asked ourselves. If they came to be alone and to make peace between them, then why should they want us about? And how much did Gabriella know of Rosalba? Certainly she seemed a wide-awake sort. Did they have coke jags together at night?

116

"Believe me," Pieretto had said, "those two hate each other."

"Well then, why do they live together?"

"I'll find out."

It was a good thing that at table Poli never ceased filling our glasses with wine. Gabriella drank too, sipping slowly, turning her head to one side like a bird at the end. I thought: perhaps if we all drink enough they will become more sincere, more like children, and Gabriella will tell us that despite everything she likes her Poli, and he, Poli, will say that Rosalba was homely, that she had become a bad habit, an infatuation, and that our encounter had cured him, our encounter and Oreste's cry. Nothing more would be necessary, I told myself, to make us immediately closer friends, we would leave Pinotta in peace and take a walk together or go to sleep contented. Life on the Greppo would be changed.

"I'm afraid you're going to be bored," said Gabriella suddenly. "All we have here at nights is crickets. Your friend did right to escape. . . ."

"The crickets and the moon," Poli said. "And us."

"So long as they'll be happy . . ." Gabriella said, toying with the rose before her. She raised her eyes, intent. "I hear that you used to go nightclubbing in Turin with Poli?"

She looked at us for an instant and then burst into laughter.

"Come, come! Did somebody die?" she exclaimed. "We're all sinners. Misfortunes make us younger and no one is guilty of anything. We have lost a son and he is found. Let us kill the fatted calf."

Poli looked up, snorting.

"Madame," Pieretto said. "I toast the fatted calf."

"Madame? . . ." she said. "Don't call me madame. We could even call each other by our first names. We have enough common acquaintances."

Poli's face clouded and he said: "Listen, Gabri. We're going to end up like last night."

Gabriella smiled faintly, maliciously. "There's no music," she said, "and no one is drunk this evening. All the better. We can talk sincerely."

Pieretto said: "We can drink later on."

"If you want music," Poli said, getting up. "I'll put on a record."

I saw her slender hand squeeze the rose and let it fall, and I didn't dare look into her face.

Poli had already sat down, not having put on the record. "Music requires happiness," he said. "First let's drink a bit more." He held the bottle out to fill her glass.

Gabriella accepted the wine and drank. We all drank. I thought of Oreste and his vineyards.

After we lit cigarettes in the silence, Gabriella inhaled and then looked at us and began to laugh. "We haven't understood each other at all," she said mockingly. "Sincerity is no crime. I hate *crimes passionelles*. I should only like to know if Poli was very ridiculous that night in the car when he discovered the sincere life. . . ."

18

"Let me talk," Gabriella cried. "When two people live together, they speak so little, and each knows what the other will reply. When two people live together, it's like being alone. . . . I should only like some one to tell me if—you two were there that night—if Poli told everybody about his innocent life. . . . He discovered it at Turin—I know that. And I'd like to know what you two looked like while you were listening to him. For Poli is sincere. Gabriella said with conviction, "Poli is ingenuous and sincere as a man ought to be, but sometimes he forgets that everyone doesn't have crises of conscience. That's what's nice about him,"—and she smiled—"his being ingenuous. But tell me what you looked like when he was explaining all that."

And she planted her eyes on us, hard and laughing, malicious.

Poli did not become discomposed at this turn in the conversation. He had an air of expecting quite something else. It was Pieretto who said: "White furore with foam. The gnashing of teeth was heard. Some one had seven devils in him."

I didn't like Poli's face. He looked at us out of swollen and half-closed eyes, his face twitching.

"*Quos Deus vult perdere . . .*" Pieretto continued. "It does happen, you know."

Gabriella looked at him, astonished for an instant and then laughed faintly, a foolish laugh. Her mood changed

The Devil in the Hills

suddenly and she proposed: "Shall we go out and get a breath of air?"

We got up in silence and descended the steps. The noise of the crickets and the odour of the sky met us.

"Let's go look at the moon from the woods," Gabriella said. "Then we'll have coffee brought out."

Pieretto came to my room that night. I was excited by the thought of sleeping in that house and of waking up there the next day and then going down to find those two, talk, sit at table and spend another night together. We had sat under the pines and the moon till late: Gabriella had made no further allusions to the past; completely at ease, she made us talk about ourselves. But what really stuck in my throat was the tension, the suspicion, the things unsaid. I now knew that they were all alike, even Poli and Gabriella —all willing to bare their insides just to pass an evening. The night before, the trees and the moon must have seen black things. Why all that ambiguous talk, like ivy hiding a well, when everyone knew what well was involved?

I told Pieretto that in my room, when we were smoking the last cigarette of the evening. "Can you tell me what we're doing in this house?" I asked. "They're not our sort of people. They have money, lots of friends, plenty of time. Did you ever see anyone eat with flowers in his plate before? Oreste's vineyards were better, the cleft was better. Oh yes, Oreste realized that straight off——"

"However, you do like Gabriella," he interrupted me.

"Gabriella? When she fights all the time? She's already understood us from head to foot. Look at Oreste. . . ."

"Oreste will come back, you'll see," Pieretto said.

"I hope so. Tomorrow. . . ."

120

"Don't shout," Pieretto said. "I'm not leaving here even if they put me out. It's too good a comedy. . . . So long as it lasts."

Then we talked about Poli and his strange destiny—his gift of irritating women.

"He's a very queer sort indeed," Pieretto said. "He ought to be a hermit. He was born to live in a cell but he doesn't know it."

"One wouldn't think so. He certainly knows how to choose women."

"What does that mean? Merely that they're after him like furies."

"Yes, but he doesn't mind. Gabriella is his wife. *You* don't sleep with him."

Then Pieretto looked at me in that way of his halfway between foolish and amused.

"You're awfully stupid!" he said. "Gabriella doesn't sleep with Poli. Anyone can see that. You just have to have eyes in your head."

He enjoyed my amazement and continued: "Neither of them even thinks about it. I can't imagine why they live together."

"For the matter of that," he continued, "I daresay they don't themselves know why they live together."

I slept well in that soft bed with the silk eiderdown. To be alone after days and weeks of sleeping three in one room refreshed and rested me like the sky which I greeted the next morning from my window. Everything was awake and alive and sparkling, and the sun which filled the plain on the other side of the pines reassured me of the vastness of the horizon and persuaded me that we would do many

121

things at the Greppo, we would enjoy the woods and the company, we would talk, play, absorb that place with our whole beings. There were remote spots and glades, many long afternoons, there was Gabriella's grotto. We had already mentioned going back there.

Oreste arrived in mid-morning, ringing his bell like a postman. He was accompanied by Pinotta who had gone shopping at Due Ponti. The funny thing was that he really was bringing the post, postcards which had arrived for us; and Gabriella shouted to him from the window: "If it takes letters to bring you here, I'll tell all my friends to write to me."

We all entered the room with her and sat down to wait for Poli. Oreste, in excellent humour, told us that he had seen partridges rising about the countryside and heard whirrings and chirpings which promised early hunting.

"Do you like shedding blood so much, Oreste?" Gabriella exclaimed.

Oreste went on about hunting and said that Poli shouldn't sleep so late. The time for summer hunting is really before dawn and as much before dawn as you can manage to make it. . . .

"Not with dogs," Gabriella cried. "It doesn't do the dogs any good. The dew injures their scent." She laughed at Oreste's surprised face. "You didn't know that when I was a girl I used to spend my vacations on the Brenta among lark hunters? You couldn't hear anything but shooting and dogs baying. . . ."

"Where's Rocco's old dog?" Oreste came out.

"He must be dead," Gabriella replied. "Have you asked

Poli? By the way, Poli doesn't want to shoot any more. Did he tell you?"

Oreste looked at her interrogatively.

"He doesn't like it any more," Gabriella explained. "It doesn't fit in with the new life." She smiled. "However, he still eats meat."

"I knew it! I knew it!" Pieretto howled.

Oreste was puzzled by our high spirits, and he looked into one face and then the other, uneasily.

"We talked about Poli last night," Gabriella explained. "You really must stay on here with us. Everything happens at night here."

Later on, Gabriella disappeared. We wandered through the rooms off the verandah; there were books, card-tables, a billiard table. I liked the green light of the pines through the window. In a corner I found novels, illustrated magazines and Gabriella's workbasket. Dull sounds came in from the kitchen. I hadn't yet seen the gardener.

"With all the land you have," Pieretto said to Poli, "why don't you set yourself to digging it?"

At Poli's vague smile, Oreste said: "It takes another sort of person to do that. His father will finally sell the whole thing. He doesn't even use it for hunting."

"Why *should* he dig?" I asked Pieretto, raising my eyes from the magazine.

"A man in crisis always digs the earth," Pieretto said. "She's the common mother and plays no tricks on her children. You ought to know that."

"However," Poli said, "in September you can hunt the woods. . . ."

No one said anything. I thought that September was

near, about ten days, and wondered whether it would be right to stay so long. It seemed understood that we would remain. I said nothing and opened the magazine again.

At lunch Gabriella came down in a negligée, smelling of sun. Laughing in the shade behind the drawn shutters, she got Oreste back on the subject of hunting.

19

And that was how Oreste came to stay at the Greppo.
Sometimes he would go away on his bicycle and then come
back. The hill seemed to bake in the August sun; honeysuckle and horsemint made an invisible wall round it, and
it was pleasant to walk about there and, when you reached
the point of coming out in the neighbouring wood of hornbeams, to go back into the thicket like an insect or a bird.
You seemed to be entrapped in that perfume and sun.
During the afternoons of the first days, we used to descend
the steep slopes to the point where the vines grew smothered
in grass; and once we walked all round the hill, and, pene-
trating a growth of briars, came upon a small, black kiosk
with a half-ruined roof through the fissures of which we
could see the sky. But there were no traces of hedges or
paths; the hillside was all wasteland, for all that it had once
been a garden and the hut a pavilion. Oreste and Poli
called it the Chinese pagoda and remembered the time when
it had been covered with jasmine. Now as we approached
it among the thistles, we heard a rustle of rats or lizards—
they had taken over the hill. The thicket appeared so virgin
and wild that the contrast did not make you feel sad. Nor
were our voices among the bushes enough to violate it. The
idea that the great summer sun beating in the woods had
an odour of death was true. Here no one broke the earth
to get something out of it, no one lived on it: once they
had tried and then had given up.

Pieretto said to Gabriella: "I don't understand why you two don't spend the winter in this kiosk. You could eat roots. You could find the peace of the senses. . . . In summer the country is disgusting, it's a sexual orgy of pulp and juices. The winter is the only season of the soul. . . ."

"What's got into you?" Oreste said.

And Gabriella very angrily said: "Oh, you're crazy."

Poli smiled.

And Pieretto continued: "Let's be sincere. In August the country is indecent. What about all those seed pods? There is a musty odour of coitus and death. And the flowers, the animals in heat, the fruit that drops?"

Poli laughed.

"The winter! The winter!" Pieretto shouted. "Then the earth is buried at least. One can think of things that concern the soul."

Gabriella looked at him and at Poli, and smiled fleetingly. "I know how to spend the winter," she murmured, "and I like this indecent odour."

In the first days when Poli and Pieretto were together a great deal, Oreste and I used to go half way down the hillside with Gabriella and smoke a cigarette while sitting on the brow of a rise and looking at the minute trees in the plain.

Unlike Poli, who never said a word about the towns, hills and churches, Gabriella made Oreste point out everything. She wanted to know how the peasants lived and where Oreste had spent his boyhood, where they had gone hunting. More than anything, I liked to look off from the height towards the region of the oaks, Mombello of the red earth, where the two brothers lived. We spoke about them once when Gabriella, curious, had asked me if Oreste's girl lived there. I told her it was something better than that: two intelligent men who cultivated their vineyards and were sufficient unto themselves. Oreste said nothing. It seemed to me that when I was praising Davide and Cinto, I was talking about him, Oreste.

Gabriella had asked: "But if they're the owners, why do they do all the work?"

I began to explain to her that that was the fine thing about them, and that only if you cultivate your own land are you worthy to live on it and that all the rest is servitude. Her face was so tanned that when I saw her lips part ironically, they seemed extraordinarily red.

She said faintly: "That must be the way they're made."

Walking with them in the odour of horsemint and parched earth, I would think that we were the horizon, an island in the sky, to anyone in the vineyard of San Grato. I don't know whether Oreste thought about it, he wasn't the sort to think about it. I said jokingly to him: "If you had been born on the Greppo that would have been your horizon." I pointed to the plain where the villages showed whitely. "Don't you want to get on a ship and take a trip around the world any more?"

"There are only rice fields down there," Oreste said "and then Milan. . . ."

"Oh, Milan! Don't speak badly of Milan," Gabriella pleaded. "I have to go back there some day or other."

In those first days I still thought that I liked Gabriella and that there was nothing wrong in being near her. When we were alone—she, Oreste and I—we could talk without Poli's shadow making us uneasy. Neither he nor Rosalba would cross our minds, and if some reference to those Turin days was made, Gabriella would be the first to smile. But most of the time we talked very little: Oreste, as usual, kept silent. I wasn't sure of my ground; I felt that there was something like a withdrawal, an unnecessary pretense in her even when she laughed, clapping her hands. Perhaps Pieretto could have stood up to her, but even Pieretto went cautiously. At bottom, I liked to think about her more than anything else, to think that we were living on the Greppo and that she was living there too, that she was inhaling, just as we were, the odour of the thicket. The most pleasant times were when we went down to the grotto or the vineyards—to eat wild fruit, throw ourselves down on the grass, toast in the sun. There was always some slope, some cranny, some tangle of trees which I had not yet seen, touched, and absorbed. That indefinable odour of August, of brackish earth, was stronger there than anywhere else. There was the pleasure of thinking about her at night, under the large moon which dissolved the stars, and hearing at my feet, on every side, the secret hill which lived its own life.

Oreste pointed out to us the wildlife on the Greppo. There were magpies, jays, squirrels, and a few dormice. There were hares and pheasants. The crickets and locusts were already singing in my blood day and night, they lived and gave voice to the summer. Sometimes their noise was so loud that it made me shiver—it must have reached the serpents and the roots underground. I wondered if the owners of the Greppo, not Poli and Gabriella who were nothing, but the hunting ancestor and the gamekeepers of that day had loved this earth, this wild mountain, as it seemed to me I loved it. Certainly they had possessed it better than we had.

Gabriella's presence enabled me to understand one thing. I used to talk it over with her in my imagination as I once used to talk things over in a low voice with Pieretto. The abandonment and solitude of the Greppo was a symbol of her and Poli's mistaken life. They did nothing for their hill; and the hill did nothing for them. The savage waste of so much land and so much life could bear no other fruit than discontent and futility. I thought again about the vineyards of Mombello and the sharp face of Oreste's father. To love a land you must cultivate it and sweat over it.

We had returned to that kiosk the day after, and here Pieretto's idea that the countryside has an odour of coitus and death made me smile. Even the humming of the insects dazed one. And the stormy freshness of the ivy, the whistling cry of a partridge. I left her and Oreste on the sagging floor, where they flushed the partridges by shouting and stamping their feet, and I went out into the sun.

20

We used to spend the nights on the verandah, drinking, listening to records, playing cards.

"Is there anyone more useless than I?" Gabriella used to say. "I can't even amuse the lot of you."

She would dance with one of us and then return to sit down. The first evening we kept quiet, listening, and followed the dance steps and the blue skirt with our eyes.

"Is there anyone more useless than I?" she said one night, stretching. "I'm tired of living."

"You sound serious when you say that," Pieretto observed.

"Tired of everything," she went on. "Of waking up in the morning, of dressing, of your intellectual talk. I'd like to go to a wineshop and get drunk with porters."

"Masochism," Poli said.

"Oh, yes," she said. "I wish some one would throttle me. I don't deserve anything else."

"Oh-oh. We're having a crisis."

"Yes," Gabriella snapped coldly. "We're having a crisis. It's all the rage up here. Be careful, Oreste, or you'll be having one too."

"Only him?" Pieretto said.

Gabriella's mouth twisted. "Compared with Oreste, we're all filth," she said, including me in her glance. "He's the only one of us who's sincere and well-balanced."

Oreste looked at her so sharply that it made us laugh. Even Gabriella smiled. "Isn't it true that you don't have crises of sincerity?" she asked him. "Have you ever told a lie in your life, Oreste?"

"There are crises and crises . . ." Poli began.

"Rather!" Oreste said, happily. "Is there anyone who hasn't told a fib some time or other?"

Then Poli began to complain and to accuse us all, Gabriella, everyone, of remaining on the surface of things, of reducing life to a futile drama, to a senseless series of motions and manners. People acted according to fads and gambled their consciences on the most material and foolish things. Some on their work, some on petty vices, some on the morrow. All struggled and filled their days with words and vanity. "But if we want to be sincere," he said, "what do all these foolish things matter? Of course we're all filth. And in any case, what *is* a crisis? Certainly not getting drunk with porters, who aren't worth a straw more than we are. The only thing is to get down into ourselves and find out who we are."

"Crisis is only a word," Pieretto said.

". . . What's the good of anything else?" Poli went on stubbornly. "Everything else can be bought, you can hire others to do it for you——"

"Everybody doesn't have the means," Oreste interrupted.

"And so? . . . I said that you *can*, not that you *do*. These things never depend on us. But who you really are— that is something that no one can tell you. . . ."

"But aren't we filth?" Gabriella shot out. "Oh, Poli, hadn't you agreed that we're filth?"

"Poli is maintaining something else," Pieretto observed. "That we all tend to be satisfied if we conform to good manners and current opinion. It isn't sufficient to know

131

that we're filth, that's much too little. We have to ask ourselves *why*, we have to understand that we shouldn't be filth and that even we are made in God's image. That way we get more fun out of it."

Gabriella went to change a record. At the first notes she turned, held out her arms and sighed imploringly: "Who'll take me?"

Oreste stood up and the three of us continued to argue. Now, looking at us out of the corners of his eyes, Poli had begun to say that if God was within us, there was no sense looking for Him in the world, in action, in works. "Then if we resemble Him," he murmured, "it must be our inner selves, the internal man that is made in His image."

My eyes followed the blue skirt and I thought about Rosalba. I was about to say "This scene is something that's already happened," but I caught sight of a strange smile which illuminated Pieretto's face.

"Are you sure that's not an old heresy?" he muttered.

"I don't care," Poli said brusquely. "I'm satisfied so long as it's true."

"Are you so dead set on resembling the Eternal Father?" Pieretto asked.

"What else is there?" Poli said with conviction. "Do my words frighten you? Call Him what you like. For me, God is absolute liberty and certainty. I don't wonder whether God exists: all I want is to be free, certain and happy, as He is. And to reach that point, to be God, a man has only to touch the depths, to know himself completely."

"Come off it!" Oreste shouted over Gabriella's shoulder.

We paid no attention to him. Pieretto, a bit tight, said:

132

"And have you touched those depths? Do you go down into them very often?"

Poli nodded, without smiling.

"I always thought," Pieretto took up, "that the best way of knowing one's self was to pay in person. Have you ever thought what you would do if the Flood came?"

"Nothing," Poli said.

"No, no. You haven't understood me. Not what you would like to do, but what you would do. What your legs would make you do. Run away? Fall on your knees? Dance with sacred joy? Can anyone claim to know himself unless he has been in the straits? Conscience is nothing but a sewer; health is in the open air, among people."

"I've been among people," Poli said, his head down. "I've been among them since I was a child. First college, then Milan, then life with her. I've had a good time, I don't deny it. I suppose it happens to everybody. I know myself. And I know people. . . . That's not the way."

"I shouldn't like to die," Gabriella said as she danced by, "because then I'd never see anyone any more."

"You tend to your dancing!" Pieretto shouted.

"But she's right," he said to Poli. "However, you see God in the mirror, don't you?"

"Meaning?" Poli said.

"Matter of logic. If the world doesn't interest you and you carry God in your eyes, so long as you live you see Him in the mirror."

"Why not?" Poli said. "No one knows his own face." He spoke with a calm air which made me stay and listen.

The music stopped. In the silence, you could hear the crickets.

"The agony begins again," Gabriella said, her arm through Oreste's. "We're sick of you chaps, aren't we, Oreste?"

We all went out under the moon which had then risen enormous, and we walked down the drive. "There ought to be a night-club down there," Pieretto said. "Then we'd have some place to go."

Gabriella, who was walking ahead with Oreste, turned and said to him: "You rotter. You had better not start talking about the Flood again."

I walked between the two pairs and smelled the earth, the moon and the honeysuckle. We passed under the hedge of pricklypears. The bushes and the trees were revealed in the moonlight on the open hillsides. There was a slight breeze which seemed like the breathing of the night.

Oreste, in front, was talking about a time when he had been riding.

And behind, Poli talked to Pieretto. "There is a value in the life of the senses, in sin. Few men know the bounds of their own sensuality . . . they know only that it is an open sea. You need courage and you can free yourself only by touching the bottom of it. . . ."

"But it has no bottom."

"It is something that continues beyond death," Poli said.

21

I made fun of Oreste because he had not gone back to the village for three days and was sleeping in a first-floor room, near that of the cook. "I trust him," Gabriella had said.

Oreste came up in the morning to wake me and we smoked at the window. . . .

"I've been walking about in the woods all night," he told me.

"Why didn't you whistle? I would have come too."

"I wanted to be alone."

I made the sort of face at him that Pieretto would have made, and immediately I was sorry. Oreste lowered his eyes like a dog.

"Is there someone else involved in this?"

Oreste didn't reply and looked at his cigarette.

"Let's go up on the terrace," I said.

You got to the terrace by a wooden ladder propped under a trap-door. We had never gone up before. Gabriella sunbathed there at midday.

We passed through the hall on tiptoe. The ladder creaked damnably under our weight. Oreste stood up first on the terrace.

It was a sort of loggia open to the sky and was full of the cool morning sun. A low brick wall stood at the eaves and all round slender columns bore wooden beams which formed a pergola. On the low wall were vases of scarlet geraniums, and the whole was encircled by the dark tops of the pine trees.

"Not bad. This woman knows how to live."

Oreste looked about, perplexed. Stools and dressing-gowns of turkish towelling and a reclining chair were folded against the wall. I thought that if you sat in the open chair, you wouldn't see anything but the sky and the geraniums.

"No need to take her to the cleft, old man," I said. "She's darker than we are."

"You mean she sunbathes naked?" he stammered.

"Did she invite you up here too?" I smiled and again I was sorry. Oreste didn't take his eyes off the dressing-gowns.

"The ants and the bees are lucky," I said. "Let's go down."

Whose fault was it that morning? Mine, who was joking? And thinking it over now I blame the Greppo, the moon, and all Poli's talk. I should have said to Oreste "Let's go home." Or have talked it over with Pieretto. Perhaps Pieretto could still have saved him. But Pieretto, who understands everything, was aware of nothing those days.

As for the rest, I liked the game too. Midday approached and Gabriella, who had walked about the house all morning in shorts, had chattered, slammed doors, sent Pinotta running about—Gabriella suddenly disappeared, leaving us under the sunny pines or on the quiet verandah to read or to listen to one another by turns. Oreste and I glanced quickly at one another, it was a secret of ours, and that hour of sunlight passed in suspension, buzzingly, all too slowly. One morning when Poli went upstairs and we didn't see him for a while, I saw Oreste grow pale. I wasn't jealous of Oreste; I didn't think seriously about Gabriella; but I didn't even have to wonder whether he thought about her. I enjoyed the game, that was all; it was a secret rather like that of the cleft, and similarly innocuous; nevertheless, I was careful not to let Pieretto understand. Pieretto was the sort who would have talked about it at table.

But by the time I thought of saying to Oreste "Isn't Giacinta expecting you?" I knew it was too late. That was the morning Oreste didn't answer my usual wink: he was no longer himself. Gabriella had talked with him. They had gone out together at sunrise after a storm the previous night, and from my window I saw them come back across the grass, laughing. Poli hadn't left his room that morning; I found Pieretto and Pinotta downstairs talking, and Pinotta looked at me crossly. Pieretto said that we were back to the usual state of affairs.

"That idiot's been sniffing again."

Pinotta said that she had been called in to clean the vomit from his bedclothes.

"Has it happened other times?" Pieretto asked.

"Every time they drink too much," she said.

The evening before we had drunk only orangeade. The heavy air and the first flashes of lightning had made us restless and put us in a bad humour, which in me turned into sharp discomfort, a real sense of guilt and, shifting the conversation to our stay at the Greppo, I had said that it was time we were off. They had all jumped on me—she too—and told me that we were having a good time and that we still had lots of things to do. "The only one who has a right to complain," Poli said, "is Pinotta. But Pinotta isn't allowed to." And then, as the bright flashes lit up the pines, I said that I couldn't understand why, if they had

137

come to the Greppo to be alone, they had any need of our company.

"What presumption!" Gabriella had said, but a clap of thunder sent us inside and we didn't talk about it any more.

Now Pieretto followed me into my room and we discussed Poli's relapse.

"I was expecting it all along. That idiot's a real addict," Pieretto said. "His father wants to keep him in the country . . . . he'll be up in an hour," he continued. "There's no danger. . . . This is what happens when you're sons of God."

"If there's any need, we have Oreste here," I observed.

Pieretto smiled wryly. He was thinking about Poli. "He's completely debauched," he said. "It's the fault of this world in which fathers make too much money. And so instead of starting from the bank like all the beasts, these golden children find themselves in deep water when they don't even know how to swim. And then they drink. You know the sort of life they made him live as a boy?"

He told me a horrible story of servants and governesses with whom his father and mother had surrounded him at the Greppo until he was thirteen or fourteen. They had taught him all sorts of imbecilities, principally that the rich are born to their riches and that it was right that women bowed to his mamma. Before God, of course, they were all His children. In fact, one of the maids had taken him to bed when he wasn't yet twelve and had sucked his strength for months. Not content with that, she then took him into the woods where they played at taking off one another's clothes, so that Poli was already a libertine before he was a man. "For him life *is* these things," Pieretto said. "He used to steal his mother's sleeping pills so that he could drug himself. He chewed tobacco. He used to slap the maids so that he would have an excuse to embrace them and be hugged. . . ."

"He's the pig," I said impatiently. "What's money have to do with it? Not all his kind resemble him."

"They do resemble him," Pieretto said. "But he is different in this—even though his wife does say it—that he is more ingenuous than they. He does these things seriously, you know. You'll see him become a Buddhist, if he doesn't die first."

It was then that looking out of the window I saw Oreste and Gabriella as they arrived, laughing. They were slipping on the grassy slope and laughing.

I said to Pieretto: "And Gabriella? Does she take coke?"

"Gabriella is making fun of all of us," he said. "It amuses her."

"But why do they live together?"

"They're used to quarrelling."

"Mightn't they like one another?"

Pieretto laughed and gave a low whistle. "These people," he said, "have no time to lose. Their problems are simpler. It's always a matter of money."

Then we went down to the verandah, and I saw Oreste and I saw her. Gabriella had already visited Poli, who had a room separate from hers, and had said on returning: "The patient has risen."

No one said anything about drugs. Gabriella's and Oreste's eyes sparkled and laughed so much that we forgot Poli. We continued to argue about going to dance at a village festa the next day, a village famous for its fair at

139

the end of August. When Gabriella disappeared at midday, I glanced rapidly at Oreste, and I became aware then that he didn't want to respond. He remained seated, alone, and chewed his own cud. But his eyes were shining. Then I thought seriously about Giacinta.

22

O reste went home to get the gig to take us to the fair, but it held only three and Poli had a headache and down there in the village one had to dance. Then I said that I would stay behind at the Greppo too, for I had grown fond of it and besides a day on leave is always pleasant.

"You rotters," Gabriella said, already seated between Oreste and Pieretto. "However, it's a shame."

They left, shouting good-byes and laughing. I spent the morning at the little grotto circled with maidenhair. At that spot the brow of the hill rose against the sky and a cane-brake hid the plain. The latter was a souvenir of other times; perhaps there had been a vineyard up there. I stretched out naked at the mouth of the grotto and sunned myself. I hadn't done that since our days in the cleft. I was astonished to see how dark I was, almost as dark as the stems of the maidenhair. I thought about many things as I let my eyes wander about here and there. From the thicket which enclosed and sheltered the glade someone might come out, but who? Not the servants, not Poli. The spirits of the rocks and woods, perhaps, or some insect from the Greppo—beings as naked and savage as myself. In the clear sky over the reeds, the white sickle of the moon gave a magic, emblematic quality to the day. Why is there a relationship between naked bodies, the moon and the earth? Even Oreste's father had joked about it with us.

At noon I returned to the pine-encircled villa, old and

white as the moon. I poked about behind the house, near the offices; through a narrow window I saw Pinotta's red head bent over her ironing. While I was looking in the open door at the rich vases of variegated flowers, old Rocco came out and muttered something. We struck up a conversation; he observed that I had a good colour.

I said that the air on the Greppo was healthy and that Poli probably owed his healthiness and liveliness to the years which he had spent on the Greppo. Pinotta began to listen with her angry expression.

"Yes, yes," Rocco said, "the air. There's plenty of fresh air."

I thought that it would be a nice job if Poli made love with Pinotta too.

I had to smile because Rocco looked at me askance. Then he spit his cigarette butt into his hand, a large, black hand, and muttered something.

He complained about the season. He said that there was not enough water in the reservoir and you had to carry it. Once there had been a pump, but now it was broken.

Then I asked where the drinking water came from. "Spring water," Pinotta said from the window.

"Who draws it?"

The red head shook savagely: "I do."

I wanted to talk with Rocco, get him to describe to me the forest and life in the old times, but Pinotta's round eyes never left me for a moment.

Then I asked if anyone bathed on the terrace and where the water would come from. Pinotta snickered. "Madame *sun*bathes on the terrace," she said.

"I thought perhaps you carried water up."

"I haven't killed anyone yet."

She grew bolder and asked why I hadn't gone to the fair. This subject interested Rocco as well. They looked at me hopefully, as if they were learning a great secret.

"There wasn't room for all of us in the gig," I said shortly.

Old Rocco shook his head. "Too many people," he muttered, "too many people."

Poli, whose face was still worn from the day before, came down a moment for lunch and then went back upstairs and reappeared only at dusk. We hadn't exchanged ten sentences all day; we didn't know what to say; he smiled his tired smile and poked about. All afternoon I glanced through the old books in the billiard room, yellowed albums, old encyclopædias and collections of illustrations. When Poli came back in at twilight, I raised my head and said:

"Will they be back for dinner?"

Poli lifted his eyes and his face cleared. "I say, let's have a liqueur in the meantime," he proposed.

Then we drank, seated under the pines.

"Time flies," I observed. "Even up here where everything seems fixed. At bottom, you're well off alone, Poli."

He smiled. He wore his gold chain, and his white shirt contrasted with his bronzed skin. He asked politely about my life in Turin and what I would do when I returned. We talked about Pieretto; I told him that the women in Oreste's house had thought him a theologian, and he laughed, becoming more animated. He said that Pieretto was better than a theologian but that he had a defect: he didn't believe in the deep forces or in the callow innocence which we all have within us.

I asked if he was going to spend the winter at the Greppo. He nodded, his eyes intent.

"I keep thinking," I said, "that your being in this place where you spent your childhood must have a certain effect on you. For you, every single thing here must have a voice and a life of its own. Particularly now."

Poli kept silent, his eyes were attentive.

". . . When we arrived here, even I was moved," I said. "Imagine that. And I'd never been here before. But this mixture of abandonment and secret roots—not simple countryside, it's something more than that—struck me at once. When you used to live here, was it like this?"

He looked at me doggedly.

"The house was the same," he said. "There were more people, more servants. But they haven't changed it."

"I don't mean the house. I mean the woods, the uncultivated vineyards, this wild air. This morning I took a sunbath at the grotto, and it seemed to me that the hill had blood and a voice, that it lived. . . ."

I saw him pull himself together.

". . . You've been here a long time. Have you ever thought such things about the Greppo?"

I was talking and all the time saying to myself: "If you're a lunatic, here's another. It might even be that you'll agree for once."

Turning his glass in his fingers, Poli said: "I was crazy about animals. Like all children. We had dogs, horses, cats. I had Bob, an Irish trotter. Afterwards he broke his back. . . . I like the laziness of animals. They are freer than we are. . . ."

"Perhaps what I mean about the hill you found in animals. Did you like the wild ones too? Hares? Foxes?"

"No, I didn't like them," Poli said firmly. "I used to talk with the animals, the way I talk with you. But you can't talk with wild animals. I liked Bob because he let you give him the quirt. I liked the cats because I could hold them in my lap. Do you understand?" he said, his face clearing. "It was like being with a woman, like being with mother. . . ."

"Mother . . . she was something else again," he continued. "Poor thing, she made me suffer. There was the winter when she went to Milan and I spent Christmas alone with the servants and the snow. I looked at the snow from the window in the dark, and when the women came looking for me I wouldn't answer, so as to drive them frantic. . . ."

"That's a winter memory for you," I said.

"My mother's dead now. . . ." Poli said. "You're right. Now whenever I stay in the country, it's like winter to me."

So the evening went by, and at midnight we had to eat. Pinotta looked at the two of us seated at that table and had an air of enjoying herself hugely. She clattered in and out of the dining room. I felt a certain anxiety more than Poli did. We drank a lot and at one moment, I don't know how it happened, I spoke to him of Rosalba. I asked where she was, how the affair had ended.

"Oh," Poli said, disconsolately, "she's dead."

145

23

By the time Gabriella and the others arrived in the gig
half-way through the morning, I was dazed and hoarse.
All night we had talked about Rosalba's death. Poli didn't
know much about it. She had killed herself in that pension
run by the nuns—poison, some sort of sleeping tablets—
when he had left for the sea. We had walked under the
pines and round the reservoir and talked and talked, in low
voices, until day came. Poli said that death was nothing,
it's not us who determine it, inside us there is joy and peace
and nothing else.

Then I asked him if coke was a part of the peace of the
soul. He replied that everyone uses drugs of some sort, from
wine to sleeping-powders, from nudism to the cruelty of
the hunt.

"What's nudism have to do with it?"

Oh yes, it had a great deal to do with it: there are those
who go out naked among people for the pleasure of brutal-
izing themselves and violating a human norm.

The night wasn't long enough for me to make him admit
that there is a big difference between suicide and death by
disease or accident. Poli talked about Rosalba in the hesi-
tant voice of an impassioned boy; he spoke gently of when he
had been on the point of dying; no one was guilty of anything; Rosalba was dead; they were both well off.

All night, almost as though granting that he was right, I
drank, argued and smoked. Dawn found us in the easy

146

chairs, and Pinotta, untidy, made coffee for us. The moon disappeared behind the pine needles. We were then talking about hunting and the poor animals: Poli said that shedding blood was to him the least comprehensible of all drugs; Rosalba had taught him that blood has something diabolic in it. "Now Oreste wants to go hunting. He doesn't seem to understand that others may be repelled by it. Well, let him go, but let him leave the rest of us in peace. . . ."

The light of day calmed me a little, but I couldn't sleep for tension, tiredness and dumb anger. When I heard the happy voices in the clearing before the villa, an anger against Pieretto seized me, for certainly he had known the whole story but he had told me nothing; and so I didn't go down at once; I stared vaguely at the ceiling and thought that Rosalba, the coke, the spilt blood and the hill were all a dream, a jest, that all of them were in a conspiracy against me. All I had to do was to go down, pretend that nothing was happening, not let myself be swept into the vortex. Laugh at him, that certainly. . . .

A noise, a gunshot, made me jump from bed. I ran to the window and I saw them drop laughing from the gig. Oreste brandished a smoking shotgun. Her hair blowing in the wind and her dress tangled in the armrests, Gabriella shouted: "Help me down!"

Pinotta and the cook ran out; Poli appeared. Talk and greetings began. The wine, the fair, the brooks. "We never laughed so much," they were saying. "We stopped by at Oreste's village." The horse pawed the earth with his head lowered.

I went down too, and it was noon before the hubbub died away. They threw themselves into the chairs and shouted about one thing after another. An understanding reigned among them, the result of their having been on a binge together. They knew how to have a good time, those people, they told us. What villages! And Pieretto had been in a ditch, he had had a fight with the keeper of a wineshop; then they had rung the bells and made the sacristan come out; they had stolen grapes from a vineyard.

"And so," Pieretto said, seated on the arm of Gabriella's chair, "have you got your guns ready, Poli? The rest of us will be your dogs."

Calm returned at noon. Gabriella went upstairs to freshen up. I looked at Oreste, he was quiet and happy. You could see his developed intimacy with Gabriella hoarded up in his eyes. There was no need to ask him anything.

I couldn't make out Pieretto who had begun to joke again with Poli. They were talking about a peasant who had known his grandfather and told how the old man had got many women pregnant in those parts.

"An old family custom," Poli said. "People in the country like that sort of thing."

Then Pieretto said: "It's a pity that Gabriella likes you. She could relieve the family's debt in that respect. You ought to send her to these fairs oftener."

Whatever Pieretto had in mind, it was Oreste who exploded inarticulately. Poli raised a perplexed eyebrow.

Oreste was on his feet in front of Pieretto, but he didn't say a word. They stared at one another for a moment, both red in the face, but Pieretto had already got control of himself.

"What's bothering you?" he said sharply. "Target practice hurt you?"

148

Oreste looked first at him and then at Poli and left the room without saying anything.

Later, when we were alone at the top of the staircase, I asked Pieretto if he knew about Rosalba. He replied quietly that he had known it for some time and that he expected it ever since those days in Turin. "What do you expect a woman to do in that situation? A woman has no way out. They're incapable of abstract thought. . . ."

"Poli's a thoughtless bastard. . . ."

"Didn't you know that?" he said. "Where have you been all this time?"

I could have punched him. I bit my tongue. At that instant, Gabriella went fluttering by in the hallway; she threw us a greeting and ran down.

"What's this new mess?" I murmured. "Which one of you seduced her?"

"You mean, who thinks he's seduced her. The cock robin who'll seduce her hasn't been born yet."

"However, someone's really taking the whole situation seriously."

"That may all be so," Pieretto said, laughing sarcastically. "Have you given him this advice?"

I realized then that Pieretto was more innocent than I. I took him by the arm—a thing I had never done before—and we went to the window. "There are three days left," I said, "and some sort of mess can still develop. I told Oreste that it would be better if we went away. As far as I'm concerned, they can kill themselves. Poli means nothing to me. . . . But Oreste does."

"What are you scared of? The gun?" Pieretto said, ready to laugh.

149

"Anyhow, I notice that you've had the same idea. What scares me is that you can't talk with Oreste any more. . . ."

"Is that all?"

"And I don't like Poli's expression. I don't like the way he talks. I don't like this story about Rosalba. . . ."

"But you do like Gabriella."

"Not when you get drunk in ditches. These people aren't like us. . . ."

"But that's what's interesting about them," Pieretto exclaimed. "That's what's interesting about them."

"You said yourself that they hated each other."

"Don't be an ass," Pieretto said. "At least people who hate each other are sincere. Don't you like sincere people?"

"But Oreste's supposed to marry Giacinta. . . ."

We continued until they called us downstairs to lunch. We found Poli perplexed and irritated, Oreste cantankerous, and Gabriella with her hair washed, chattering about the red tassels on the oxen and the abominable smell of carbide lamps.

"I like the smell of carbide," Pieretto said. "It reminds me of the winter booths and the horns in Turin."

24

I wanted to talk with Oreste. It wasn't that he avoided me, but he had an air half-way between the sarcastic and offended which discouraged me. I stopped him on his way down the stairs and asked him to show me his gun.

"Can we come hunting with you?" I asked.

He had thrown his gun and game-bag on a divan in the billiard room.

I took a red shell from the bag and said: "You want to kill Poli with one of these?"

He took it from my hand and muttered: "What the devil are you talking about?"

Then I asked him to let me talk. In a low voice (the others were nearby on the verandah) I told him that inasmuch as we had got to know Poli so well, it was our duty to treat him like a friend. Did he think that he was treating Poli like a friend? Suppose that two weeks before, Poli had started to pay attention to Giacinta, who wasn't even married, what would have happened? At the least, he and Gabriella should know enough to hide the affair. Some fine day even crazy, thoughtless Poli would no longer be able to shut his eyes to it. Wouldn't it be better if we left at once, went home and kept a pleasant memory? What did he hope to get out of it?

Red-faced, Oreste listened to me and was on the point of interrupting me many times. But when I stopped talking, he smiled a stubborn smile and kept silent, looking me up and down.

"It's not the same thing," he stammered finally. "Certainly I'm not stealing anything from anyone. And we don't want to hide anything. She agrees, too."

"Of course she agrees. She's a woman. But how will it all end?"

He looked at me again, his mouth contracted wryly. "They'd been separated for over a year," he said. "She never wanted to see him again; it was Poli's father who sent her here. Because he wanted to keep Poli in order, so that he wouldn't get into any more scrapes. You've seen the way Poli treats her. . . ."

I didn't answer him by saying that you don't cure a sick person by making him drink or making him angry or making love under his nose. It was useless, for Oreste spoke indignantly, with that stubborn redness that means "Now or never."

"She's an extraordinary girl," Oreste said. "You should have seen her at the fair dancing and laughing and joking with the musicians. . . . She knows how to talk to all sorts of people. . . ."

"And did she tell you that you're the man for her?"

Oreste made an effort and looked at me. He looked at me quickly, with an air of indulgence. His eyes shone. Days later, when it had become clear that the whole thing was bigger than all of us, I realized that his glance had been an attempt not to be insolent, not to offend me with his happiness. Because things like these made us ashamed. We didn't know how to talk about them.

"For the matter of that," Oreste said, "even Poli knows. After the Turin affair. . . . She had already separated from him. . . ."

"Did she tell you that? . . . . Well, then, why are they living together here?"

We continued like that until they came and interrupted us. I didn't manage to disturb him or to get him to relax his persistence. Gabriella must have realized that we were talking about her, for she came and took us by our arms and said: "Come on, you chatterboxes." And all the time she examined me closely.

That afternoon we went hunting. Poli came along too. "We'll talk and they can shoot," Pieretto said to him. It seemed to me that Poli was watching Oreste and his wife with an amused air. Now and then he would stop for a bit, detaining Pieretto and me, he told us how wonderful it was that of all the acquaintances he had made in recent years none understood him like us two. I let Pieretto talk; at one point, becoming impatient, I turned off behind a large thicket. I knew that Gabriella and Oreste would have to go down as far as the vineyards to find pheasants, I knew that Gabriella wasn't thinking about pheasants, nor was Oreste, nor Poli. Then I decided to remain alone, to find some bank, some giant reeds and the horizon. I did so and then lit my pipe.

Yes, it was hard not to see Gabriella, not to hear her talk, not to be in Oreste's place. I asked myself if during my last talk with him I had shown him any spite or rancour. The thought that she could go willingly through the wood with one of us, even into the Kiosk, and that together in the light of day. . . . I recalled the Po, I recalled the cleft. Where was the summer's odour of death now? And where all our chattering, all our conversations?

A gunshot sounded. I cocked my ear. Gay voices followed, I distinguished Pieretto's. Another shot. I got up and looked among the vineyards for the puff of smoke. They were lower down, almost among the hornbeams. They're a couple of fools, I muttered, they're really shooting pheasants. And throwing myself down on the grass again, I listened to the humming of things, the vibrations of the shots, the life of the Greppo which I could now enjoy peacefully.

We climbed back up the hill when the shadow of the Greppo filled the plain. They had killed about ten sparrows, which lay covered with blood in the game-bag, among the cartridges. Gabriella gave her arm to Oreste and Pieretto and made a face at me; they asked me where the devil I had got to.

"Another time they'll shoot you. Be careful," Poli said to me very calmly.

At table we talked about hunting, pheasants, of what game might be flushed. Oreste talked excitedly, with assurance, as he had not done for some time. Gabriella kept her eyes on him all the time, with a perplexed and distant expression. "Davide and Cinto have cleaned out the preserve," Oreste said. "Why don't you change your gamekeepers?"

"So much the better," Poli said. "Hunting is a sport for kids."

"And for princes," Pieretto said. "And for feudal gentlemen. That's what you need on the Greppo."

Then Gabriella curled up in her chair and listened to us

talk and didn't mention cards or music. She smoked and listened, she looked from one to the other of us and seemed to smile. Drinks came and she didn't want any. I watched Poli's face and wondered what the evenings at the Greppo were like when he and Gabriella were there alone. We would have to leave some time or other. And they would have to leave too. What was this villa like on winter evenings? A sudden pain, a discomfort, seized me at the thought that summer on the Greppo, Oreste's love, all our talks and all our silences and we ourselves would all be over in a short time, finished and done with.

But Gabriella jumped up, she stretched, yawning like a baby and said without even looking at us: "Turn out the light. Isn't it true, Oreste, that if you want to look at bats you have to turn off the lights?"

They went outside to sit on the steps, and we behind them. The sound of the crickets was denser than the stars. We talked about the stars and the seasons.

"The last morning star appears down there," Oreste said.

He and Gabriella went among the trees; they walked side by side, cheek to cheek; we could hear their rustling.

It was strange to think that Poli was seated beside us. For a moment it seemed to me that he was the only sane person: we all kept quiet, anxiously. And Poli said: "It's like the night we looked down on Turin."

"Something is missing," I murmured.

"The hunting cry."

Then Pieretto—I heard him take a deep breath—threw out that awful shout, lacerating it in his own manner and

155

then laughing scornfully. A trampling of feet in the house followed, doors creaked, and from a distance Oreste's faint voice replied.

"Let's hope Gabriella doesn't catch cold," Poli said.

"Aren't you drinking anything?" Pieretto asked.

25

"Lord! how I'd love to step into a bar," Pieretto said when we went back up the steps with the bottle. "Or walk past a cinema, spend a night in Turin. How about you two?"

Poli said: "Sometimes I wonder if women have any understanding. If they understand what a man is. . . . Either they're all over a chap or they're running away so that he'll come chasing after. No woman knows how to be alone."

"You can run into that sort after midnight," Pieretto said.

"I used to think they were sensual," Poli said, looking at the floor. "I thought that they were at least sensual. Like the devil. It's only skin deep. No woman is worth a pinch of coke."

"But doesn't the man also have something to do with it?" I muttered.

"The fact is," Poli said, "they lack any sort of interior life. They lack liberty. That's why they're always running after someone they never find. The desperate ones, the ones who don't know how to enjoy themselves, are the most interesting. . . . No man satisfies them. They are real *Femmes damnées*."

"*Dans les couvents*," Pieretto said.

"In convents, my foot," Poli said. "On trains, in hotels, all over the world. In the best families. The women locked up in convents and prisons are the ones who have found their lovers. . . . The God they pray to or the man they killed never leaves them for a moment. And they have found their peace. . . ."

I cocked my ear to a rattle of gravel. I hoped that Oreste and Gabriella would come back and that it was all over. But it was only a pine cone that had fallen, or perhaps a lizard that had scurried across the drive.

"All of which shouldn't concern you in the least," Pieretto said to Poli. "Or were you thinking of killing someone."

Poli lit a cigarette, revealing his face, his half-closed eyes. He seemed to have been taken aback. He said out of the dark: "I'm not sufficiently altruist to do that. It's a pleasure that has no attractions for me."

"He lets people kill themselves," I said to Pieretto.

We fell silent for a long time and contemplated the stars. From the coolness of the pines there rose a sweet odour, as of flowers. I remembered the jasmine of the kiosk which once must have seemed like so many stars under the shade of the wood. Had anyone ever lived in that kiosk?

"Animals understand men," Poli said. "They know how to be alone better than we do. . . ."

Gabriella returned, running. "You can't catch me!" she shouted.

Oreste came up then, more calmly. "Your flower," he said to her.

"Oreste can see in the dark like a cat," she laughed.

When we went back in and lit up, we all had hold of ourselves. We scattered about the room and Gabriella, humming, looked through the records. She wore an oleander flower in her hair. She relaxed in a chair and listened to the song. It was a sweet blues, syncopated, a piercing contralto. Oreste stood silently by the gramophone.

"That's a nice song," Pieretto said. "I never heard it before."

Gabriella smiled, listening.

"Is it one of Maura's records?" Poli asked.

That was how the evening ended, and we went to bed. I slept badly. Pieretto waked me, entering my room when the sun was already high.

"I have a headache," I said.

"You're not the only one," he said. "Listen to them; they're already at it."

The sound of the record, the contralto's voice, filled the house.

"Are they crazy? At this hour!"

"It's Oreste greeting his love," Pieretto said. "The others are sleeping."

I washed in the basin. "Isn't Oreste overdoing things?"

"Nonsense," Pieretto said. "Poli's the one I can't understand. I didn't expect him to complain, but you'd have said that he wouldn't like to be cuckolded."

I was combing my hair and stopped short. "If I've understood rightly," I said, "Poli's tired of women. He said that they don't let him breathe. He prefers animals or ourselves."

"Not in the least. Don't you realize that when he talks about women he suffers? He's an ass, he's in love. . . ."

When we got downstairs the song had been over for some time. Pinotta, who was dusting, told us that as soon as Oreste had put the record on, he left in the gig saying that he would be back at noon.

"He's not got a grip on himself any more," Pieretto said. "Now we're for it."

"He'll be back on the bike."

Pieretto laughed at that and even Pinotta looked at me impertinently.

I couldn't keep it back. "I wonder what effect the station will have on him?" I muttered.

"It'll be good for his health, it'll be good for his health," Pieretto said, rubbing his hands. Then he turned to Pinotta and asked: "Did you remember the cigarettes?"

At eleven, not being able to resist any longer, I went upstairs and knocked on Poli's door. I wanted to ask him for an aspirin. "Come in," he called. He was in a canopied bed, wearing handsome claret-coloured pyjamas, and Gabriella was seated at the window, dressed in shorts.

"Excuse me."

She looked at me amused.

"This is visiting day," she said.

There was something jammed. I didn't like their faces.

She stood up to get the aspirins for me. She crossed the polished red tiles and searched about in a drawer. "If I'm not mistaken. . . ." she said, laughing into the mirror.

"They're in the bathroom," Poli said.

Gabriella slipped out of the room.

"I'm sorry," I faltered. "We didn't sleep the other night."

Poli looked at me without smiling, bored. I had the feeling that he didn't see me. He moved his hand and only then was I aware that he was smoking.

Gabriella returned and handed me the vial. "We'll be right down," she said.

I spent the morning at the grotto with my headache. I

wondered if, from Gabriella's loggia, one could see the cane-
brake where I was hidden. I thought about old Giustina
and Oreste's mother and what they would have said if they
knew what was happening at the Greppo. But I felt calmer
that morning; it seemed to me that the most difficult matter
had been accepted, that everything could still be adjusted.
"That rotter," I said to myself. "He's already got a girl.
You can see what sort he really is."

After I went back up the hill, I found no one and I
stopped under the pines. I wondered if Oreste had returned.
The level top of the Greppo smoked among the pines, in
the rays of light. Every time I came back from those walks
I thought that it would be the last. But since Poli didn't
throw us out, it meant that he still managed to stand us;
and if Pieretto had been right, Poli would have sent us
packing long ago. He was always the same, Poli was: he put
up with Oreste so that he could have Pieretto and me
around to help him talk and pass the time.

Unfortunately Oreste had arrived. Pieretto said: "They're
sunbathing up on the terrace," with an innocent air, and
Poli, beside him, apparently paid no attention. His face was
drawn and it seemed that he hadn't slept much. He was
smoking, holding his cigarette in an unsteady hand.

"They're sunbathing on the terrace?" I stammered.

They looked at me as you look at a bore. They began to
talk about God again.

But Poli said something at lunch. He complained that
one of us had put a record on at seven in the morning. He
blamed Gabriella for having wakened him. He said harshly:
"There's a time for everything."

Gabriella looked at him ferociously. But Oreste, who

161

regretted what he had done, jokingly declared that he was the guilty one.

We all fell silent and Gabriella glanced round hotly. She was really furious. "To have to live with lunatics and children!" she said disgustedly.

Then Oreste, red-faced, threw down his napkin and went out among the pines.

26

There followed a painful afternoon of silence. Oreste's absence sent the hunting party up into the air; Gabriella retired to write letters; Pieretto said, "That fool" and went off to take a nap. The only calm person seemed to be Poli, who remained in the drawing room leafing through magazines, a bottle of cognac beside him. Seeing me pass by the window like a soul in torment, he asked why I didn't come in and have a drink and call Pieretto. Then I moved back in the clearing before the house, shouted Pieretto's name and went off.

I went down to the hornbeams and then beyond. It was the first time I had gone that far. I found myself on the red path leading to the plateau, dusty, scattered with cow-flops. A swarm of yellow butterflies danced above it. That hot odour of clover and stable was pleasant, it reminded me that the world wasn't coming to an end on the Greppo. Turning over all my piques and irritations, I decided to announce that evening that I would return to Turin.

Going back up the path, I looked at the hill for the last time. From below you could see only the pines and the slopes covered with shale and thickets. The Greppo really was like an island, a useless, untamed place. At that moment I should have liked to have been far off, thinking about the Greppo while living my usual life. That was how much that hill had got into my blood.

I met Rocco who was walking slowly down the path. He told me that they were looking for me.

"Who?"

From what I could make out, all four of them, and they were very quiet. They were having tea under the pines.

"The doctor too?"

The doctor too.

They're crazy, I thought, and I came out on the top of the hill circumspectly. Gabriella, in a red skirt, shouted when she saw me, shouted that I shouldn't be unfaithful to her, that I shouldn't desert them as I had yesterday. I shrugged my shoulders and then sipped my tea. Oreste, as though nothing had happened (he still had his gun across his knees), again began to explain certain fine points of shooting. Then we went off.

This time we all descended in a group. I touched Pieretto's elbow and questioned him with my eyes. Pieretto hunched up his shoulders and looked at the sky. "But weren't they running away together?" I whispered.

"She went into his room," he replied.

Then I went up beside Oreste and said: "Where's this hare that we're supposed to kill?" Then Poli said something to him and he turned round, and Gabriella glanced at me fleetingly with a twisted smile. As we had already left the path, we quickly found ourselves alone behind a bush. My heart beat rapidly as I stammered: "May I talk with you a moment?"

"I beg your pardon?" she said, laughing all the while.

"This won't do, Gabriella," I said. "I wanted to talk with you about Oreste."

We had stopped walking. I saw her eyes close to mine. She was serious and yet laughing.

"Oreste's a great trial," she sighed. "Oreste is being very bad."

At my glance she shrugged her shoulders, moving off. She spoke firmly. "You must tell him that, if he pays attention to what you say. You seem to be good friends. He shouldn't do these silly things any more. I'm not afraid of chaps like you. . . ."

We walked among the trees and underwood. The footsteps of the others followed behind. Pushing aside some branches, Gabriella took my wrist and breathed: "You don't know how much I care for him. . . . No one knows. So serious and funny and young. . . . No one knows. . . . Don't you dare tell him I said this. . . . But he must obey me and not do silly things. . . ."

We came out into the sun, and the others came out too. Something brushed past my head and a shot sounded. I heard Pieretto shout something. Gabriella shouted too. We all shouted. Oreste had shot at a duck, a wild duck, he told us—and he had missed.

"That was bright, shooting at our heads," Gabriella said. "You might have killed us."

But Oreste was gay. "It's only bird-shot," he said. "You'd have to catch a man pointblank to kill him with bird-shot."

"Give me the gun," she said. "I want to shoot."

Poli had remained at the edge of the glade, almost as though to divorce himself from the hunting. We waited for another bird to fly by; Gabriella held the gun over her arm; Oreste looked from her to the sky, excited and happy. After nothing happened for a bit, Poli proposed that we move on to the kiosk.

That evening at table, we talked and joked about the wild duck.

"You need a dog for proper hunting," Oreste said.

"First you need a hunter," Pieretto said.

They both ate and talked excitedly.

"I see you haven't lost your appetite," I said to Oreste.

"Why shouldn't he be hungry?" Poli said. "He's a hunter."

"He's a growing boy," Pieretto said.

"What have you all got against Oreste?" Gabriella shot out. "Let him alone. He's my man."

Oreste looked at us with a mixture of confusion and gaiety.

"Look out," Poli said to him. "Gabriella's a woman. . . . Have you noticed that Gabriella is a woman?" he went on lightly, jokingly.

"That's not hard," she laughed. "I'm the only one here."

"The only one," Poli said, and winked and smiled.

Pieretto had an air of understanding everything and of having a good time. I saw Oreste lower his head and eat. It seemed to me that he wanted to hide himself. And Gabriella looked at him a moment, without changing her provocative smile.

For how many days had Gabriella smiled at him like that? She smiled at me too; even at Poli. It seemed like those first days on the Greppo. She and Oreste would disappear, they would go up on the terrace together or into the wood. It seemed that they were playing; there was no need to hide. I believe that they would have been able to meet and talk under our eyes, even under Poli's: Gabriella was the sort to do it. At times I should have said that she was laughing at us, that she was using Oreste only to rid herself of the rest of us. When we found ourselves round the table in the evening, Oreste looked surprised and frequently stunned. Neither Pieretto nor I succeeded in discouraging him, not even by mentioning Poli. In any case, what did it matter? For Gabriella, he was only a pastime. I told him so one evening when I saw him with a wrinkled forehead, and Oreste shook his head as if to say "You don't know."

Now and then they would have arguments, fought out with silences and glances. In the mornings, when Poli was late coming down and Gabriella found Oreste everywhere under foot, she would tell him to keep us company, to go and get some flowers, to accompany Pinotta to Due Ponti. "Go 'way, you big baby," she would say. She would say it, annoyed, with a quick smile, as she would pass through the rooms. Oreste would go out under the pines, desperate. But Poli would come down, Pieretto would come down, and then Gabriella would call him peremptorily, she insisted that he be there too, she would take his arm. Oreste would obey, under Poli's sarcastic glance.

27

"**I** don't like this pinewood very much," Pieretto said one evening, approaching it with Poli. "It's not wild enough. You don't find any toads and snakes."

"What's got into you?" I said.

"I'll bet that you're having a good time," he said; he smiled sarcastically. "The cleft was better. You can't even stretch out naked here. It's too civilised."

"It doesn't seem so to me," Poli said. "We're living like peasants."

Gabriella came out among the trees and looked at us suspiciously.

"What are you up to?" she asked.

"If only we were up to something," Pieretto said. "Poli here is convinced that we're living like peasants. I thought that we were eating and drinking like pigs. All right—like gentlemen, then."

"Gentlemen?" Gabriella said sarcastically.

Then Pieretto laughed at her. "People have strange ideas," he said. "Do you think that you're earning your livings?"

But Poli said: "If you want to sunbathe in the nude, you may."

"Impossible," Pieretto said. "One feels far too civilised here."

"You want to go naked?" Gabriella said. "Why not? . . . . But peasants don't do such things."

168

Then Pieretto looked at me. "Did you hear that? Madame has your ideas."

"Don't call me madame."

"The fact is," Pieretto said, going on obstinately, "that no one succeeds in going naked as animals do. I wonder why? . . . ."

Gabriella smiled faintly.

"Understand, I mean living naked," Pieretto said. "Not getting undressed just for the fun of it."

Oreste appeared among the trees with an expression of having been offended.

"I believe that we're all naked without knowing it," Poli said. "Life is weakness and sin. Nakedness is weakness, it's like having an open wound. . . . Women know that when they lose blood. . . ."

"Your God must be naked," Pieretto muttered. "If he resembles you he must be naked. . . ."

We sat down to table embarrassed. Not even Pieretto joked that evening. Oreste, who was looking very sadly at Gabriella, seemed to me the most innocent. Something of the conversation under the pines had remained in the air, something that made us ashamed. Suddenly I was aware that Poli and Gabriella were exchanging glances, hard, almost anxious glances, truthful. The old impatience seized me, the desire to be alone. It was Pieretto who spoke at this moment.

"We are at the last dregs of the pleasures of the Greppo," he brought out sharply. "What do you say, Oreste?"

Surprised with a tender expression on his face, Oreste raised his head. But no one smiled. Neither Poli nor

169

Gabriella raised any objections. It was clear that something was happening. I thought again about Rosalba.

"Hunters, the season is over," Pieretto said then.

Oreste smiled timidly.

"There are the other seasons," Gabriella said suddenly, with unexpected vivacity. "Woodcock and partridge." She became sulky. "First you have to collect the vintage."

Then we talked about that again—it was the thorn in Oreste's side. There was the understanding with his father that we were to be present at the vintage at San Grato. We had discussed it at the time, and as always when we mentioned it, Oreste's face darkened.

"It's a shame that the vineyards of the Greppo will be harvested only by the thrushes," Poli said, looking closely at him. "Cheer up, Oreste. You go on down and we'll wait for you."

But, strange to say, it was the uneasiness which weighed on the dinner that removed the ill-will from our glances. The sound of a klaxon burst into the silence which followed. A flash of light swept across the window panes and Gabriella was already on her feet, animated, exclaiming: "It's them! They've come back." We heard loud voices and shouting. The sound of the klaxon resembled Oreste's hunting cry. Poli got up from the table, quite put out. Pinotta crossed the room to run to the kitchen. At a certain moment I was standing alone with Oreste, and I remember that I poured out a drink, I don't know why, while outside the laughter and the noise increased; I put my hand on Oreste's shoulder and said: "Buck up, old man."

That was how the night which was to have been our last began. Outside in the mild, starry air, there reigned an

odour of pine trees and ripe countryside. The brutal light
from the headlamps of the two cars threw the gravel, the
black trunks of the trees, the emptiness of the level top of
the Greppo into magic relief. Milanese were popping out
everywhere. Gabriella casually introduced me here and
there; blinded by the lights, I shook hands; Pieretto shook
hands; when we went back inside I didn't know anyone.

Our dinner was upset. Pinotta, who usually served us in
a lace apron, reappeared wearing her lace cap as well. They
opened the liquor cabinet. The men and girls threw themselves into chairs amid laughter and protests; this one had
already eaten, that one had drunk. Baskets came in from
the cars, a flood of things, bottles and sweets; corks flew. I
counted three girls and five men.

The women were in travelling clothes, with scarves round
their faces, an arabesque of colours and bare legs. None
could touch Gabriella. They talked loudly, asked for matches,
looked at us squarely. Names crossed, I heard the name
Mara. There was a lean young man with a demoniacal
face and a strange jacket that only reached his waist. They
called him Cilli and as he entered he gave a glance at
Pinotta which made everyone laugh. Another took Gabriella
by the arm and they dropped onto a divan. Still another,
standing apart, took charge of the tumult in an accom-
plished manner, shouting greetings to everyone.

While they were getting over the excitement of meeting
there, it was impossible to talk of anything else. The refer-
ences to Milan, the repartée and the common excitement
caught up even Poli, who made a great to-do over the
women, winked and answered them volubly. Gabriella, her
face flushed, argued with those nearest her. They all pro-

171

tested, almost in chorus, against the hidden life of Gabriella and Poli, the immoral egoism of love in the country and deliberately sought boredom. A man in a light-coloured suit, with a strong, ironic face—a certain Didi, about forty, as I learned later—took advantage of a moment of silence and coldly declared that one has affairs with other men's wives, never with one's own.

Pieretto sniffed the ambience like a hunting dog. I became aware that Oreste had disappeared. Gabriella had disappeared. They came back immediately, carrying a small table. Pinotta came with lowered eyes, carrying a bucket of cracked ice. Laughing, Gabriella clapped her hands—I realized that she had changed her dress and was now in blue—and she suggested that whoever wanted to freshen up should go upstairs. Four or five of us remained on the verandah, including a thin woman seated next to Poli.

28

The thin girl said to Poli: "Tell me now why you're living 'way up here."

"Don't you know?" Poli said. "My father is keeping me prisoner."

The thin girl made a face. Then she wasn't so much a girl as you first thought. She held out a glass and said: "Give me a drink." She had a hard, bored voice, and her fingers were covered with rings.

"Your father or Gabriella?" she said, laughing foolishly.

"It's the same thing," said a young man with mussed hair, seated on the arm of the divan. "They're both family obligations."

Then Pieretto opened his mouth. He said: "You couldn't get the secret out of him in a whole evening."

No one paid any attention to him. The young man said: "But we want to amuse you. We thought that perhaps being here alone you might not be drinking enough. We're here to show you how. Didi's bet that you don't even know what they're dancing in Milan this year."

"Here," Poli said seriously, and he raised his finger and beat the time.

"No!" they all laughed and shouted. The thin woman coughed, striking her teeth against the rim of her glass. The ironic-faced Didi came in, showing his gold teeth.

"You're a year behind the times," said the young man when he could make himself heard.

"Not more than three months," said the impassive Didi, as though he were leading the conversation. "Poli has an arrested development of three months."

Didi was bronzed and had cold eyes, and he spoke carelessly, in a self-assured manner. I was thinking again about Poli's ill-humour when he had heard them arrive and of the glances that had previously been exchanged. Now everything was upside down and people entered the room, burst in from the stairs; there were all the well-mannered faces again. Gabriella entered last, when the gramophone began to scratch.

I was resting against a window sill and I wanted to disappear, to escape into the wood. Imperturbable, Pieretto had already begun to chatter in the group. No one was dancing yet. The lean Cilli entertained himself all alone, wolfing down sandwiches with a great bobbing of his Adam's apple. Oreste had disappeared again. I looked at Gabriella. She was saying something to Poli, and the young man with the mussed hair was pulling her by the wrist. She was laughing and talking and let herself be pulled along. She was beautiful in that dress. I wondered how many of those men had touched her, how many knew her as Oreste did.

I didn't like the other women. They were just so many Rosalbas. Slumped down in their chairs, blonde or dark, they laughed coldly and exchanged toasts. The thin one, beringed and wearing more make-up than the others, hadn't yet moved. She listened to the conversation of the men, her small, intent face innocent and corrupt at the same time. She was curled up on the divan with her legs under her.

Then suddenly I saw everyone dancing. The contralto's voice sang those blues. Oreste was still missing. Gabriella was dancing with Didi, who didn't even then lose any of his indifference. It was evident to me that he was her sort of man. He murmured something, and Gabriella laughed against his cheek.

I crossed the room to get a drink. I found Pieretto eating bits of ice. "You still on your legs?" I said to him.

He looked at me tolerantly.

The strange Cilli approached, making his way through the dancing couples. I expected some joke—expected him to make faces or imitate a rooster. Instead, he held out his hand. "Delighted," he said in a stupid voice.

"Pleasant place," he winked.

"Is this the first time you've been here?" Pieretto asked.

"I don't know exactly where we are," he said, again with that stupid voice. "We were at the club playing poker and some friends came by and picked us up. I thought we were going to the casino, then I saw Mara and she told me we were going to Poli's. And who the devil remembers who Poli is? . . . . They tell me he's crazy." He rolled his eyes in imitation of a madman. "How's the maid?" he whispered. "The redhead. . . . Edible?"

"Edible as strawberries," Pieretto said.

"What do they say about Poli in Milan?" I asked.

"Who the devil knew he was alive? . . . . He's just a good excuse for a drive."

He had turned to the door with his birdlike gestures. He pulled his jacket at the waist and left.

"Elegant and sincere," I murmured to Pieretto.

Pieretto shook his head and looked at the table and the couples. "They're all sincere," he said as though he believed it. "They eat, drink and attack one another. What do you expect? Do you expect them to teach you how it's done?"

"Where's Oreste?" I asked.

"If you were one of that crowd, you'd do just as they do. . . ."

I had another drink and went outside.

It was pleasant to walk out into the night and stop at the brow of the hill. The music and the noise died away behind my back, leaving me isolated in the emptiness of the countryside, which seemed to float among the stars.

When I went back in, I took Gabriella aside. "Oreste is waiting under the pines," I told her.

"He's crazy. . . ."

"I don't know which of you is crazier," I said. "As for me, no one is waiting for me."

Then she laughed and ran out.

Now and then a circle would form and Pieretto would hold forth, laughing loudly and teasing the women. No one had yet suggested that they all go out under the pines. The tireless gramophone sang. At bottom, it was easy to mingle with these people. Both the women and Didi wanted only to have a good time. All you had to do was to have a good time with them. The morning was still far off.

The most constant dancers were Poli and the thin woman with the rings. There came a time (I don't know how long Gabriella had been out) when the gramophone went silent. Poli and the woman stopped dancing and held each other tightly. The others formed a circle round Cilli, who, kneeling on the carpet, howlingly prostrated himself before a portrait of Poli on the floor. Pieretto was in the circle, not yet satisfied.

Suddenly Cilli began the litanies. Mara, Didi's blonde friend, dried her eyes and begged him to stop. The others clapped. Poli approached weavingly and he laughed too.

But Pieretto said something. He said that a real god has the mark of a wound between his ribs. " Let the accused bare himself," he declared. "Let him show us his wound."

You heard one or two timid laughs, then everyone fell silent and didn't laugh any more. The thin woman, who was outside the circle, breathed hard: "What is it? What are they doing?" I didn't dare look at Poli; the one scarlet face was enough.

Someone put on a record; couples formed immediately. I found myself drinking beside Didi, who turned round looking for someone. "She isn't here," I said. "She'll be back right away." He raised his glass, with a half-wink. I nodded very seriously. We had understood one another.

The Devil in the Hills

I was very drunk. The noise and the music seemed to cloud the room for me. I saw Poli seated at the far end. Someone was talking to him—and he seemed calm, a bit done in. He was pale, but by this time everything appeared pale.

Gabriella and Oreste came in.

29

Now many had gone out under the pines. They talked about making up a hunting party and beating the hillside. They were looking for someone, Poli, I think, and the girl with the rings. The gramophone fell silent. I went inside to get another gin.

Oreste passed by and clapped me on the shoulder. He was happy for some reason or other.

"Things going all right?"

His hair was mussed too.

"These asses," he said. "Why the devil don't they go home?"

"What does Gabriella say?"

"She can hardly wait to send them packing."

Gabriella went out at that moment with Didi. "Good," I said; "now you've got to drink."

Cool, almost cold air came in the window, for the season was so far advanced that now the plain was covered in mist every morning and evening. Pinotta passed under the magnolias with a tray, and in the shadow someone grabbed her. It was Cilli. She gave a quick, strong jerk and ran off, letting the glasses fly. At the crash, a chorus of cheers burst out among the pines.

"You see," I said to Oreste, "tonight they're getting their bellies full. Where's Pieretto?"

"I wish they'd leave."

We were alone on the verandah. "Now you can tell me," I murmured into my glass. "Were you up on the terrace with her? Were you?"

Oreste looked me frankly in the face and scarcely moved his lips. I leaned forward. Laughing, he shook his head and went off.

I heard low voices and a cough on the staircase. That was the way to the bedrooms. Perhaps they were even going into mine. I couldn't hold myself back and went into the hallway. No one. Then I went up the stairs, ready to smile casually. Lights were blazing all over and gave me a sense of solitude. No one upstairs either. Then I entered my room, closed the door behind me and switched the lights on and off. No one. I sat down to smoke in front of the window, in the dark. I heard shouts, indefinite voices and rustlings from the direction of the pines. I thought of the no longer virgin Greppo.

Footsteps in the corridor startled me. I went out and saw the blue skirt turning round the corner to go down. I caught up with her halfway down the stairs.

We descended together and Gabriella only made a face at me.

I said: "Tired?"

She shrugged her shoulders.

I didn't ask her about Didi.

I went outside too. I heard feminine shrieks and Pieretto's rasping laugh. "They're having a good time," I said.

Dropping down on the steps, Gabriella took me by the hand and forcibly pulled me down. "Stay here a minute," she said to me in a conspiratorial tone.

"Suppose Oreste came," I muttered.

"Would that bother you?" She smiled. "Do you want a drink?"

"Listen," I said. "What have you been up to with Oreste?"

She didn't answer but kept hold of my hand. I could hear her breathing and smell her perfume. I leaned against her cheek and turned and kissed her.

She moved away. She didn't say anything, but she moved away. I hadn't touched her mouth. She hadn't replied to me. Now my heart was beating so hard that she must have heard it too.

"Silly ass," she said coldly. "You see? . . . . That's what I was up to with Oreste."

I felt mean, and at the same time desperate. I listened to her with my head lowered.

"You're just kids," she said. "Oreste too, and that other chap. What are you after? We're friends. But it stops there. This winter you'll be back in Turin. Oreste has to go back too. You must tell him that. Oreste has a girl and I hope he marries her. I've got nothing to do with it."

"I kept silent. After a bit, I stammered: "Are you jealous?"

"Oh, come off it! That's the last straw."

"Then it's Poli who's jealous. . . ."

"Don't talk nonsense. All you've got to do is to tell Oreste I'm not a free agent. Will you tell him that?"

"What's the matter? . . . . You're crying!"

Her voice was thin. "Yes. . . . Tell him I cried. He's got to understand that Poli is sick and that all I want is for him to get better."

"But Oreste says that you didn't know what to do about

181

Poli. You separated. . . . Where were you when Poli was in hospital?"

I was ashamed of having said that. Gabriella kept silent. My heart was beating rapidly again.

"Listen," she said, "will you believe me?"

I waited.

"Will you believe me or not?"

I raised my head.

"I'm very fond of Poli," Gabriella whispered.

". . . ."

"Does that seem very absurd?" she demanded.

"And is he fond of you?"

Gabriella stood up and said: "Think it over. You must tell Oreste. . . . After you've left you must repeat it to him every minute. . . . You're sweet."

She went off under the pines. My head was in a whirl. When I got up, I felt like running down the Greppo, I felt like walking and walking until dawn, until I reached Milan or somewhere, as I used to do those wild Turin nights. Instead I went back into the room to get another drink.

Then Poli approached from the stairs. He had two jackets thrown over his shoulders and his eyes were like ash, like embers in ash. I expected him to be drunk, but not like that. He told me to stay with him, to sit down and smoke with him. He spoke in a low, insistent voice.

I asked him politely if he had known these friends long. And then I realized that he was not drunk. Not with alcohol, at least. His eyes looked as they had that night we met him on the hill.

"Poli," I said, "don't you feel well?"

He looked me up and down and his hands gripped the arms of his chair.

"It's getting cold," he said. "If only it would snow at least. Oreste could kill something. . . ."

"Are you angry with Oreste?"

He shook his head, not smiling.

"I wish you chaps would stay here always. Aren't you having a good time tonight? You don't want to go away, do you?"

"Your friends from Milan are leaving tomorrow morning."

"They bore me," he said. "Old, worn-out people who don't know how to talk." He gave a heave, like a person retching, and pressed his lips tightly together. He lowered his eyes and continued. "It's unbelievable . . ." he said. "The oldest soul that is inside each of us is the youngest—the soul we had when we were boys. It seems to me I've always been a boy. It is the oldest habit that we have. . . ."

Some idiot outside sounded a klaxon and the raucous, strangled noise made Poli jump.

"The trumpets of Judgment Day," he said darkly.

Didi entered at that moment. He saw us and stopped short. "That beast Cilli," he exclaimed. "He's got hold of someone's panties and he waves them under your nose and says that if you can guess whose they are, the woman is yours. Now I ask you. . . ."

Poli looked at him dully.

"Are you drunk?" Didi asked. "Is he drunk?" He assumed his ironic smile again. He rubbed his hands and went to the table. "It's chilly," he announced. "I don't know what's got into the girls." He emptied his glass and

183

clicked his tongue. "Anyone upstairs?" Poli looked at him, still dully. "Have you seen Gabriella?"

After Didi went off, Poli took up: "It's nice to shout that way in the night. . . . You know . . . as you did on the hill. . . . It seems like an underground voice. It seems to come out of the earth or out of the blood. . . . I like Oreste."

30

Dawn found us all in the room, in twos and threes or slumped alone in chairs. Cilli and another chap were sleeping. One girl stared at the windows, another babbled on aimlessly. Pieretto and Didi were sipping *grappa*.

We had returned one by one, from the thicket, the wood, the brow of the hill. Pinotta, whom I knocked up, made coffee for us.

The yellowish faces became blue and then pink in the dawn, and the electric light paled. When we switched it off we looked about apprehensively. The women were the first to liven up.

They left in clear daylight, on the damp gravel which made little noise. Old Rocco, standing beside the reservoir into which he had dropped the end of a rubber hose, watched them leave.

"We'll be back," they called. "We can make it in good time on the highway."

"We'll be coming to Milan," Gabriella shouted from the crest.

Poli had already gone back into the house. We wandered listlessly on the gravel, looking around. A chequered scarf hung from the low branch of a pine. My foot struck a glass on the gravel, unbroken. Now, in the morning, in the ordinary light, I didn't dare catch Gabriella's eye. Even Oreste, walking with his hands behind his back, was silent.

"Stupid people," Pieretto said. "Milanese."

Gabriella smiled tiredly. "Don't be banal. Perhaps they say the same of us."

"It's the men's fault," Pieretto said; "you know what sort a man is by the women he puts up with."

Oreste said: "You don't put up with them."

"Listen," Gabriella said, "settle it among yourselves; I'm going to freshen up. Peace be with you."

She went off in the clear air. We went back into the room. It seemed impossible that we would be able to take up the life of before. Something had changed. Who would have thought so? It was as though we had already left.

An odour of stuffiness and flowers hung on in the disordered room. I smelt burning wax. A cigarette smoked slowly in a saucer.

"Last night I found Pinotta crying in the kitchen because no one ever takes her dancing," Oreste said.

We remained seated in the chairs. I expected a headache and I got one.

"Hair of the dog," Pieretto said. "That's what you need." He poured out a glass.

Then we spoke about going to shop at Due Ponti. We liked the idea. "That way we'll help out Pinotta."

I went up to my room to get my jacket. As I went through the corridor—bright with curtains and sunlight—I heard a coughing, a spitting, a sort of death-rattle. It came from Poli's room. I put my hand on the doorknob and the door opened. Poli, sitting up in bed in his pyjamas, raised tired eyes. In his hand he held a handkerchief full of blood. He carried it to his mouth.

I stopped irresolutely, and Poli looked at me out of his swollen, defenceless eyes.

"What is it?" I stammered, breathing hard.

He made a movement as though to hide his hand and then instead he opened it. His hand too was covered with blood. "It's not vomit," he said. "Gabriella. . . ."

I found her in her room. She ran out, slipping into her negligée. Poli greeted her with astonishment, with the sulkiness of a child who has been punished. He said: "It doesn't hurt. I only spit it up."

We called Oreste and Pieretto. Gabriella moved quickly and nervously about the room, round Poli's bed. All the glances, words and gestures of recent days burned in her eyes like a fever. She did not lose her hardness.

Oreste, silent and obliging, gave Poli an auscultation, biting his lip.

"We'd better go," I said to Pieretto. "We'll leave them alone."

"Did you know he was tubercular?" he asked when we were on the verandah.

"It's not surprising, the sort of life he's led," I remarked. "Probably he knew. . . ."

"Knew, my foot," Pieretto said. "When you know, you take care of yourself."

Sometimes Pieretto was ingenuous. I told him then that you didn't always think of your health when it was a matter of doing or not doing something. I told him that Poli, for all that he might be a bit mad, was a melancholy man, a man alone, one of those who know beforehand what their lot is from the sheer force of thinking about it. "Did you know about Gabriella?"

"What?"

"That she's in love like a schoolgirl."

187

He admitted that it was so. But then he said: "What little bird told you?"

They all came down, even Poli. His eyes sunk in his deadly pale face, he seemed annoyed more than anything else. He told us in his usual voice that there was no reason for changing his habits, that the world is full of people who get nose bleeds, that those who want to live, live the way they want to.

Oreste icily explained that the disease must have been very old, and he couldn't understand how it hadn't been noticed when he was in hospital. He spoke without looking at Gabriella. "You've got to be examined at once," he said. "You'll have to go to Milan."

Then Gabriella told us that she was going to Due Ponti to telephone. "I'll go on the bike," I suggested.

"Take me along too," Gabriella said. "I want to talk with his father."

But I didn't know how to carry a passenger downhill and so it fell to Oreste, as was proper. They left, and Oreste held her between her arms with his cheek on her shoulder.

"Shall we have a drink on it?" Poli said, going back in the house. "So much for that."

He took a drink. His face was yellow and he smiled. I thought of that night on the hill when the green car had come out under the trees.

"My father. . . . That's the last straw," Poli said. "All the better that it will soon be over."

Pieretto shouted that he shouldn't talk nonsense.

"Will that change anything?" Poli said submissively. He coughed and touched his mouth. He took out a cigarette.

"Put that down," Pieretto said.

"You too?" Poli said, but he put it down without lighting it. "The day is made up of a string of little sins. You gamble your life on some little bad habit, on something unimportant. . . . There is a lot to learn."

"The world is big," said Pieretto and tossed off his glass.

When Oreste and Gabriella got back, we were a little tight, and Poli stammered out that it is easy to live when you know how to free yourself from illusions.

Oreste advised him to rest for the trip. Gabriella took his glass from his hand and told him to lie down. Then they began to go through the house, she and Pinotta, and to send us here and there, empty drawers, pack up. Oreste followed her with clenched teeth.

A little after midday the green car arrived, driven by a young man in uniform. The *commendatore*, he said respectfully, was not in Milan. Gabriella had him put the luggage in the car.

We ate in silence. Gabriella had to leave the table to give orders to old Rocco. Alone, I went to sit on the brow of the hill and look at the plain, the wild slopes. Large white clouds moved slowly in a mild sky, and there was an odour of fruit in the air.

We got into the car. We three sat in the back. Poli said nothing and I was surprised that he didn't take the wheel. Oreste's gun was slung over his shoulder, and he held his bicycle on the footboard.

I forgot to turn round when we got to the bottom of the Greppo. There was a discussion over giving the chauffeur directions. After a few minutes' jouncing we were at the station, among the flowered houses, before the familiar hills.

It seemed to me that I had always known them. We got out at the level crossing. The branch road began there, with kerbs and low hedges, a white, cement road. We exchanged a few words and joked, Gabriella's hard face smiled an instant. Poli waved his hand.

Then they left and we went to the Mill to drink.